Behind the pine, the hunter was pushing a shell into the big gun. Jubal knew that he could not make it back to the boulders before the man fired, so he waited for a target.

It came only seconds later. The skin hunter hurled himself sideways even as Jubal fired, his rifle smashing sound through the quiet evening air. Jubal felt something pluck him up out of the snow as his own rifle crashed. Searing pain lanced through his body, driving hot splinters of agony into his mind as he crashed into the welcome cold of the surrounding snow. . . .

Jubal Cade's quest for the scarfaced one takes him to the rugged, snow-covered Colorado territory, where he saves a Cheyenne brave from ruthless buffalo hunters. As he is relentlessly drawn in to the Indians' struggle to preserve their sacred tribal lands, his private death feud takes a back seat to the brutal, bloody VENGEANCE HUNT of white man for red.

Also by Charles R. Pike

Jubal Cade / 5

Vengeance Hunt

Charles R. Pike

CHELSEA HOUSE
New York, London
1980

Chelsea House Publishers
Harold Steinberg, Chairman & Publisher
Andrew E. Norman, President
Susan Lusk, Vice President

A Division of Chelsea House Educational Communications, Inc.
70 West 40 Street, New York 10018

CHAPTER ONE

Jubal Cade levered a second shell into the breech of the Spencer and sighted carefully on the first rider. He squeezed the trigger gently and felt the ·30 calibre rifle kick against his shoulder. The man he had chosen as his target screamed as the bullet smashed into his chest, carving a bloody red hole through his lung so that he coughed crimson froth out over the snow as he toppled from his horse. He fell heavily on to the sparkling white ground, the blood spurting from his shattered torso staining the snow bright scarlet.

Behind and to either side of his corpse, his three companions kicked their mounts into clumsy action, their passage hampered by the clinging, knee-deep snow as they sought to scatter and confuse the marksman crouching above them.

Jubal had watched their approach from the shelter of two boulders fronted by the splintered trunk of a fallen pine. The four men had been trailing him for over an hour now, following the clear-cut tracks etched into the snow in a relentless pursuit that was out of all proportion to the insult they felt Jubal had offered them. Like their quarry, they were dressed in heavy buffalo coats against the icy cold of the Colorado winter and two of them carried the huge ·50 calibre Sharps carbines favoured by buffalo hunters. The third held a Winchester wrapped in greasy cloth as a protection from the frozen air.

Their breath came in misty gusts as they fanned out in a ragged semicircle, warily eyeing Jubal's vantage point.

Two of them found cover behind the big pine trees flanking the trail and Jubal sighed with resignation. There was little defence he could put up against the fire power of the buffalo hunters' guns: the big Sharps were capable of smashing bullets clear through the fallen trunk that protected him. And the massive guns could outrange any escape attempt he might make, thus cutting off his path to the higher, tree-covered ground at his back.

Like it or not, he decided, he would have to shoot it out. He glanced at the pony stretched shivering in the snow where he had pulled it down out of the line of fire.

'Horse,' he murmured, a tight grin exposing his broken front teeth, 'the next time I start playing the Good Samaritan, kick me in the head. Otherwise I'm liable to lose it.'

He rested the barrel of the Spencer on the tree trunk and aimed at the man with the Winchester. The buffalo hunter was trying hard to run through the snow to the cover of a boulder protruding up through the blanketing whiteness. He never made it. Jubal's shot took him in the shoulder, spinning him around so that he dropped his rifle and pitched backwards. He twisted over on to his stomach and began to crawl forwards leaving a smear of blood behind him. Jubal pumped the action of the Spencer and sent a second shot into the man's head. It smashed into his right ear and Jubal could see blood and brain matter spew out over the snow on his left side. The buffalo hunter grunted like a hurt animal and fell still, his shattered skull held together only by the woollen scarf wrapped around the broken remnants of his cranium.

Jubal ducked as a bullet from one of the Sharps carbines echoed noisily off the boulder to his left.

'Injun lover!' yelled the man who had fired. 'How d'you feel about them now?'

'We're just good friends,' Jubal shouted back, snapping off a quick shot as a second ·50 calibre slug blasted splinters from the pine trunk above his head.

'Tom an' Joe was friends of ours,' bellowed the other marksman, 'an' they're both dead.'

'Better red than dead,' Jubal retorted.

He had known that the great buffalo herds of the High Plains country represented rich and easy pickings for the cut-throat bands of white men eager to blast the huge animals out of existence for the money offered for the buffalo hides. And while the hides were shipped East, the carcasses were left to rot until only the bones remained. So the buffalo hunters waged a constant war with the Indians of the Plains

6

who relied upon the animals for food, clothing, tents and even bone for weapons. He had not, however, realized until earlier that day the extent of the buffalo hunters' hatred of the Indians. Or that their hatred was so easily transferred to anyone showing the slightest degree of sympathy for the tribesmen.

Jubal had been riding northeast, heading for Cheyenne when he had spotted the hunters' camp. He had smelled it first, the rank odour of decaying flesh carrying even in the frosty winter air. But he had been tired and hungry and looked forward to resting awhile by a fire with a mug of coffee and talk with the first human beings he had seen in two days.

Instead he had found four men laughing at the naked Indian whose feet were thrust into the glowing embers of the campfire. In spite of the intense pain he must have suffered, the Indian retained a stoic silence as the giggling white men capered around him.

One had spotted Jubal riding up and waved him cheerfully into the camp.

'You're just in time, stranger,' he had laughed, 'the injun's got a hot foot an' now we'll warm the rest of him.'

Jubal had not bothered to dismount. Instead, he had swung the Spencer out of its scabbard and levered the action.

'Guess I don't like the games some people play,' he had said, aiming the rifle at the man's chest, 'let him up.'

The buffalo hunters had gaped in disbelief, unable to comprehend that anyone would care about an Indian, but conscious of the pointed rifle and cold command in the even voice of the small man in the buffalo coat and grey derby. Reluctantly they had untied the Indian and thrown his buckskin clothing at his feet. Without a word, the Indian had dressed and swung on to his pony. His impassive black eyes had given no hint of the pain he must have felt as he stood on his raw feet. Then he had galloped away, his only comment on the incident a hand raised, palm outwards, as he eyed his rescuer.

Jubal had been left alone, covering the four angry hunters and wondering how far he could get before they shot him down from behind. He had weighted the odds in his favour by ordering the men to throw their rifles and side arms far out into the snow and then forcing them to remove their boots. He had gathered the footwear and ridden out of the camp for a mile or so before he dropped the boots.

It had at least given him a start long enough to find reasonable cover.

The trouble was, he mused, that the start was not long enough and the cover inadequate when his attackers were using buffalo guns. He had not been looking for trouble, but he was emotionally incapable of standing silent as he watched a man tortured.

The result had been a detour into the mountainous country to the west of his path, where he hoped to elude his pursuers. But the hunters had proved too well-versed in the art of tracking their quarry and too determined to kill the man who had interrupted their sadistic sport. Now Jubal was caught in the high snow country, pinned down by the murderous fire that was smashing chips of rock and splinters of wood from his hiding place.

The buffalo hunters were taking it in turns to fire. One loosing off a shot as his companion reloaded, forcing Jubal to stay constantly alert as the heavy calibre bullets racketed around him.

He spaced his own fire carefully, moving from one side of his natural redoubt to the other so that his attackers were never sure where he would be positioned. But he was aware that he could last only as long as his shells held out: when they were gone he would be defenceless.

He eyed the stand of timber above him on the snow-covered slope and cursed as he decided that he would stand no chance of reaching the trees. Then he had an idea. Dusk was approaching and neither Jubal nor the two skin hunters would survive the cold night without a fire. He crawled to one side of his position and studied the terrain below. The hunters had tethered their horses to fir trees on either side of the trail and the rattle of gunfire had made the ponies nervous. Jubal took careful aim at the nearest animal and sent a shot smashing into the branch around which the reins were draped. The horse squealed and bucked and then, as a second bullet whined over its head, yanked the leather thongs free and cantered away down the hoof-flattened slope.

Its owner swore volubly and stumbled after it. Jubal grinned wolfishly and squeezed the trigger of the Spencer.

'An enemy in need is a friend indeed,' he murmured as the bullet hit.

The buffalo man screamed as Jubal's shot smashed his knee. His leg twisted under him, sticking out at a crazy angle as he fell headlong into the snow. Jubal hugged cover as the other man triggered a shot in his direction, then risked exposing himself to loose another shot at the wounded man. He was sitting up in the snow, dragging his smashed leg around so that he could bring the Sharps to bear on Jubal's position.

'Damn you, injun lover,' he screamed, pain lending a hysterical note to his voice, 'I'm gonna kill you.'

Somehow he got to his feet, bringing the rifle up to his shoulder as he balanced precariously on his one good leg.

Jubal grinned as he sighted. 'Mister, you don't have a leg to stand on.'

His second shot hit the breech of the Sharps, exploding the cartridge in a sudden thunder of detonated cordite and flaming gunpowder. The buffalo hunter screamed as his hands were torn apart by the blast. His arms flailed the air, sending cascades of bright red blood fountaining across the snow from the raw stumps of his wrists.

'Look,' Jubal muttered, 'no hands.'

He triggered a shot at the remaining hunter as the wounded man toppled over into the snow. He lay kicking and screaming as his shattered wrists pumped out his life on to the stained whiteness. His partner was shocked into silence by the sheer horror of the moment. He crouched silently watching the dying man paint the snow red as his writhing limbs sprayed blood in all directions. Gradually his frantic movements slowed as the severed arteries drained his body. Around him a great crimson circle soaked into the snow, turning dull red as it was absorbed, and finally he was still, face down and somehow smaller in death than he had appeared in life.

Jubal took advantage of the lull in firing to move back to the far side of the two sheltering boulders.

'You want to call it quits?' he shouted. 'Your friend's dead and that makes it tough.'

'That'll be the day,' the remaining buffalo hunter yelled back. 'Tobe may be finished but I ain't.'

He triggered a shot that ploughed snow high into the air where Jubal had previously been crouching. Jubal answered with a bullet that clipped splinters from the tree holding the man's horse, causing the animal to rear in sudden panic. The skin hunter recognized the danger of losing his mount and called softly, trying to soothe the frightened animal without exposing himself to Jubal's deadly fire.

Jubal's own pony remained where he had left it in the sheltering cover of a rock, its forefeet quickly bound with a short length of cord when he had first pulled it down. He was warily conscious of the danger of finding himself without a horse when night fell and, noting the darkening sky, realized that it was not far off.

He peered around a boulder, pulling swiftly back as the big Sharps boomed out. Rock splinters spattered into his face as the heavy bullet ricocheted high into the air.

The situation, he realized, had reached a murderous impasse. He was pinned down as firmly as was the buffalo hunter: neither man could move without risking a bullet and they would both freeze to death if they remained in their present positions for much longer. Already Jubal's hands were numb with the cold and he could feel particles of ice frosting his lips and eyes. He was not sure how long the pony could remain in the snow without suffering serious effects and if he stayed where he was he doubted that the Spencer's action could withstand the freezing temperature.

The buffalo hunter seemed to be thinking the same way because he squeezed off a shot that blasted long shards of wood from the pine tree in front of Jubal and hurled himself towards his horse. He fell in the deep snow and began to roll down the slope, clutching his rifle as he went.

Jubal triggered a fast shot that lifted tufts of hair from the man's coat and then realized that the Spencer was empty.

10

He dropped back behind the protective cover of the rock and hurriedly pushed fresh cartridges into the breech of the converted rifle. The man was still floundering on as Jubal came around the boulder, levering a shell into the breech of the gun. He reached the cover of a pine as Jubal fired, the shot slashing a ragged gash from the bark of the tall tree. Jubal was pumping another cartridge into the rifle when the boom of the big Sharps rang out.

He felt the bullet whistle past his head as he powered himself sideways into the snow. Rolling on to his knees, he squeezed off a shot without aiming and saw the other man's horse plunge madly against the restraining reins as his bullet seared its neck.

He was in the open now and knew that only his skill with the Spencer could save him from the sheer firepower of the heavy Sharps. He levered the rifle's action with desperate speed, sending a volley of bullets ricocheting off the buffalo hunter's sheltering tree.

Behind the pine, the hunter was pushing a shell into the big gun. Jubal knew that he could not make it back to the boulders before the man fired, so he waited for a target.

It came only seconds later. The skin hunter hurled himself sideways even as Jubal fired, his rifle smashing sound through the quiet evening air. Jubal felt something pluck him up out of the snow as his own rifle crashed. Searing pain lanced through his body, driving hot splinters of agony into his mind as he crashed into the welcome cold of the surrounding snow.

CHAPTER TWO

Even as he fell Jubal was pumping another cartridge into the Spencer, and despite the pain flooding through his body he twisted around so that he landed on his back. He was sitting up when he saw the horsemen, his rifle lifted to his shoulder ready to fire again. Then he saw the buffalo hunter stagger out from behind the pine tree.

Four arrows were sticking out from the man's chest and three more from his back. He had dropped the Sharps and his hands were clawing desperately at the feathered shafts protruding from his body.

Jubal watched as he walked slowly away from the big tree, dragging his feet painfully clear of the snow. He reached for the bridle of his horse but as he did so, an arrow pierced his hand, pinning it to the trunk of the pine. He was beyond pain now, moving only by the sheer animal determination of his will, and he stared blankly at the shaft sticking out of his palm. He sighed once and slumped against the pony, sending it skittering in fear away from his sagging body. Then he crumpled into the snow, tearing his hand free as he fell. It left a long smear of blood, bright against the frosted tree trunk, meandering down the bark to join the crimson pool slowly spreading around his body.

Jubal watched as the man died, aware of the pain gnawing at his own body. The horsemen sat their mounts in silent watchfulness beneath the spreading shadows of the big trees. The evening snowfall frosted their plaited hair, dusting the eagle feathers they wore with a crusting of white.

Then one kicked his pony forwards to Jubal's position. He came up slowly, the pony lifting its hooves high as it negotiated the steep, snow-covered slope. The rider carried a bow in his left hand, an arrow notched and ready to fire. Jubal sighted down the barrel of the Spencer but as his finger

12

tightened on the trigger black oblivion clouded his eyes and the rifle slipped from his hands as he collapsed sideways into the snow.

He came to in total darkness. The rank odour of half-cured animal hides was all around him and he could hear the low murmur of voices and the sounds of men moving. Somewhere a pony whinnied softly and a guttural voice speaking a language Jubal could not recognize quietened the horse. Cautiously he began to stretch his right hand out into the surrounding darkness, but the sudden pull of a rawhide thong told him that his wrists were bound, limiting movement to an absolute minimum. As his eyes grew slowly accustomed to the darkness he could make out his surroundings. He was stretched out on the ground, his wrists and ankles tied tightly to wooden stakes driven into the earth. They were too solid to pull loose and the rawhide that held him allowed only enough movement for him to twist his head to either side as he probed the blackness with searching eyes.

His clothing had been removed so that he lay, spread-eagled and naked, on the ground. His weapons, the Spencer and the Colt he had had rebuilt in Laredo,* were gone. His muscular torso was bathed with sweat and he was conscious of a dull pain in his right side, just below the ribs. He was inside a tent, its hide canopy giving off the smell that was causing his nostrils to contract defensively. Combining with that odour was the powerful aroma of burned herbs emanating from a large earthenware jar close beside his head.

He was, he realized abruptly, inside a tepee, presumably one that formed part of a village. He remembered vaguely that Indians out raiding slept rough, so the tepee must constitute part of a larger, more permanent band. And he must have been brought there by the Indians he had seen kill the last buffalo hunter.

He wondered what his own fate would be.

He was tugging experimentally on the rawhide thongs when the flap that formed the tepee's opening was pushed aside. Jubal saw the glow of a fire and outlined against the red glare, the silent figure of a brave. The Indian watched

* See – Jubal Cade: Killer Silver

13

him for a long moment and then turned to call over his shoulder.

A second brave pushed past him into the tepee, a long-bladed hunting knife clutched in his hand. He stepped over to Jubal's prone figure and knelt down beside the white man. The knife swung forwards, flashing across Jubal's face as the Indian slashed through the restraining thongs.

'Satanka say you healed now, white eyes, so you come eat.'

There was something familiar about the man's dark, flat face. Jubal sat up, rubbing his chafed wrists and remembered: it was the Indian he had saved from the buffalo hunters' fire.

'Thanks,' he grinned, 'I guess you picked me up after the fight.'

The Indian's teeth flashed white in the malodorous gloom.

'You save me from buffalo killers. I save you. The big gun hit you. You die in snow if we leave you there. So we bring you to camp.' He smiled again, 'Anyway, you kill buffalo men. That makes you friend of the Cheyenne.'

'And there's some people say the only good Indians are the dead ones,' remarked Jubal as he rose unsteadily to his feet. 'I'm glad you stayed alive.'

The Cheyenne indicated a bundle of clothing stacked in a corner of the tepee. It consisted of Jubal's grey, English-cut suit, worn across so many long, pain-filled miles since he bought it back in London,* his matching grey derby and his boots. Laid atop the pile were his gold hunter watch, the Spencer rifle bequeathed him by a long-dead friend and the Colt revolver, remodelled to take the same ·30 calibre shells as the Spencer.

Wondering at his good fortune, Jubal shrugged into his pants, pulled on his vest and hung the shoulder rig he favoured over a standard gun belt beneath his jacket. He checked the load in the Colt, slipping fresh cartridges into the chambers and then levered the action of the rifle until the gun was empty. He reloaded the converted carbine, draped his buffalo skin winter coat around his shoulders and followed the Indian out into the camp.

* See – Jubal Cade: The Killing Trail

He was met by a ring of impassive faces that stared at him from around a big central fire. He spotted the Indian called Satanka and found himself urged to squat between that brave and his new-found friend.

Fortunately several of the Cheyenne could speak English and Jubal quickly learned that the man he had saved was called Little Bear and enjoyed a considerable reputation as a brave warrior. Satanka was a healer, one of the Cheyenne's leading medicine men and a potent force within the tribe. Jubal had checked the wound in his side before leaving the tepee and could vouch for the Indian's medical skill. Fortunately the bullet had torn straight through his body without hitting any vital organs or shattering bone. The chief danger had been from the shock of the buffalo gun's enormous impact and the secondary likelihood of poisonous infection. Satanka's herbs and poultices had alleviated that risk and Little Bear's prompt action in bringing Jubal back to his camp had saved him from bleeding to death in the snow.

He had been there, they told him, for three days. It had become necessary to tie him down when delirium set in, but now he was over the worst of the wounding and, with rest and food, would speedily regain his usual good health.

'We came when we heard the guns,' said Little Bear. 'I brought the Dog Soldiers to kill the buffalo men who steal our food and take our lives. They were gone from their camp so we followed the tracks. Then we saw you shot. We killed the last one and brought you into camp.'

'Thanks,' said Jubal, chewing on a piece of meat that had been offered him from a steaming cauldron hung over the central fire, 'I guess you saved my bacon.'

'I taste bacon once,' replied Little Bear, 'white man's food. Not so good as dog.'

'Dog?' Jubal asked. 'You eat dog?'

The doubt that was forming in his mind was quickly answered by the Indian's smile.

'Yes,' he said, 'like you eating now. Special stew for brave guest. I killed the dog myself.'

Jubal gagged and swallowed hurriedly.

'Now I know why they say it's a dog's life,' he muttered.

He wondered how long he would have to stay in the Cheyenne camp. His brief examination of the wound in his side had made it clear that he would be unable to ride for some days without the risk of opening up the hole and bleeding to death somewhere on the open plain. And in winter, with settlements few and farther between than he cared to contemplate, he wanted to recover fully before attempting the long, lonely ride north. Still, he decided, time spent around an Indian village could well prove valuable. There was a great deal he could learn from the native inhabitants of the American continent, knowledge that was not available to many white men. And, he thought, the Cheyenne had so far proved useful friends. He had encountered raiding bands of Comanche and Sioux in the past* and fought them with the cold, deadly skill that made him so able a killer, but he had never mixed with Indians at close range. It could well prove a useful experience.

In any event Jubal had little choice: his wound was sufficiently serious as to render any thought of riding impossible for some time. And with winter setting bleakly into the mountainous country he would stand small chance of surviving for long out in the open.

He had originally planned to travel up northeast from Laredo to St. Louis, but the offer of a post as doctor with a Mormon wagon train heading for the Great Salt Lake and the near-legendary city Brigham Young was building there persuaded him to make the big detour that had swung him due north into the Rockies, dividing Utah and Colorado. He had left the wagon train somewhere along the Green River as it swung north along the Old Spanish Trail, bound for the Mormon's promised land. Jubal had never quite adjusted to the idea of a man having more than one wife and the three men on the wagon train who had enjoyed the company of two or – in one case, three – women, had always seemed somewhat unnatural to him. He was still attuned to the idea of one man for one woman, and the memory of Mary remained too fresh in his mind for him to easily countenance the taking of a second wife, let alone two.

* See – Jubal Cade: Double Cross

In fact, he thought as he glanced around the Cheyenne village, his memories stayed hideously fresh. He came awake, even now, with Mary's bullet-shattered face before his eyes and saw again the grinning man who had gunned her down like a cast-off dog.

He had come close to killing the man, even learned that he was called Lee Kincaid, in the Sangre de la Muerta mountains across the Rio Grande from Laredo.

It had been that doubt that had driven Jubal to join the Mormon wagon train. His wife's killer had vanished in the devastating collapse of the old mine shaft in Blanco canyon. Yet Jubal could not be sure that the man was dead. He had been smashed into unconsciousness by the falling tunnel, brought down by his own gunfire, and he had no way of telling whether or not Kincaid had died in the shaft or managed, somehow, to escape.

So he had left Laredo and the medical practice he had built up there, intending to ride to St. Louis where young Andy Prescott was staying in the Lenz Clinic. Jubal had felt both a duty and a kinship to the boy ever since the youngster had lost his sight in the savage battle that robbed him of his parents when Jubal and Mary had first headed west. Now Andy was a resident in the St. Louis clinic, totally dependent on Jubal's monthly payments of $300, which – unless they ceased – guaranteed him bed, board and the attention of the finest eye surgeon in America. Consequently Jubal had a double duty. He was determined to destroy the killer of his wife and keep Andy in the clinic until such time as he regained his sight or learned enough to live with his blindness; if, Jubal reminded himself, it should prove incurable.

However, he was committed to the dual hunt for Kincaid and the money necessary to keep Andy in the Lenz Clinic. That had been one of the reasons he had accepted the Mormon wagon captain's offer of a position with the train. It had guaranteed him a small wage in addition to bed and board and by swinging off to the East when the train reached the Green River he had planned to ride across country to Denver. The wage offered by the Mormons had been sufficient to purchase a ticket on the Kansas Pacific Railroad that would bring him to St. Louis faster than he could have reached it on horseback.

He had not seen Andy in some time, although he had been sending regular payments to the clinic and those, added to the poker winnings he had amassed in Laredo, ensured the boy's care for some months to come. None the less, Jubal felt a need to see the youngster again and he had hoped to spend some time in St. Louis before looking for work.

Instead, he had chanced upon the buffalo hunters and collected a bullet hole for his pains.

It was a vicious twist of fortune, but Jubal accepted it with the cheerful stoicism he had been forced by circumstance to adopt. His wanderings across America had taught him to maintain a near-Oriental calm in the face of adversity and he had learned to adapt himself to most situations, turning them to his own advantage.

Now he looked around the ring of cheerful Indian faces. The Cheyenne warriors seemed perfectly content with their winter camp, their dog stew and their unexpected guest. Little Bear was telling — and not, Jubal suspected, for the first time — how his new white friend had saved him from torture and how he had killed his attackers with near-Indian skill.

Jubal could understand nothing of the Indians' guttural speech. Indeed, most of the time it sounded like a collection of differently pitched grunts, punctuated by clicking sounds and accompanied by elaborate gestures. But Satanka translated for him, explaining that Jubal was being described as a mighty warrior, a seeker of justice for all men and a true friend of the Cheyenne. He could not help wondering how he would have been described had he stopped Little Bear and his braves from torturing a white man, but was still grateful that the Indians appeared quite willing to accept him for the superman of Little Bear's story.

'I guess,' he thought, 'that it's all in the eye of the beholder. And anyway, there's no point kicking a gift horse in the mouth, even if he is wearing buckskins and he's called Little Bear.'

Satanka was apparently prepared to adopt Jubal into the tribe there and then. He had learned that the white man was

18

a doctor and was anxious to pick up as much knowledge as he could of the strange medicine of the whites. As the evening drew on it became increasingly clear to Jubal that these Indians were anything other than the painted savages of popular belief. Rather, they seemed cheerful, friendly people, forced to commit acts of savagery by the ever-growing hordes of settlers, buffalo hunters and railroad men encroaching upon their traditional hunting grounds. Several chieftains had made reasonable and fully justified appeals to the white authorities. But reason and justice had little to do with the whites' need for land or their lust for the rich pickings promised by the buffalo herds and the gold deposits that lay within the Indian territory. Consequently, with the full approval of the Government in distant Washington, the maxim of the dead Indian being the only good one had been speedily adopted and the Indians were hunted and shot down with the thoughtlessness that would more adequately go with a rabbit hunt.

There were, of course, white men like William Bent who had established a trading post on the Arkansas River – it was now known as Bent's Fort – and proved himself a friend of the red men. Two of his sons had even been in the Cheyenne camp at Sand Creek when Colonel John M. Chivington's rapacious Colorado Volunteers had opened fire on the peaceful tepees, slaughtering the Indians with a sadistic brutality that far outstripped any atrocities the Cheyenne might have committed. Unfortunately, there were far more white men who followed Chivington's vicious line of thought than there were like Bent or Jubal himself.

As the Indians talked, long into the wintry night, Jubal listened to Satanka's and Little Bear's translation and found himself coming more and more to the conclusion that the whites were the villains of the piece, rather than the Indians.

The campfire was fading as Jubal shared out the last of his cherished cheroots, wondering when he might get hold of more, and announced that he was tired. As a fellow doctor, albeit unqualified by white standards, Satanka supported his claim. The Indian insisted upon examining Jubal's wound himself, but gave way to Jubal's insistence that ointments from his black medical bag should be applied rather than

19

the Indian's herbs.

Jubal was now pretty sure that the herbs were natural medicines and intended to question Satanka on their appearance and usage, but preferred for the time being to stick with his own remedies. Satanka was fascinated by the contents of the bag and studied each bottle and surgical instrument carefully, his English stumbling over the unfamiliar medical terms Jubal was forced to use in describing their purpose.

He watched with professional care as Jubal bathed the wounds in his side with iodine, then applied an antiseptic salve before covering the two holes with wadded lint, held tight by a bandage. Finally, however, both doctor and medicine man were satisfied and Jubal was allowed to retire. He refused as gently as possible the suggestion that he share both Satanka's and Little Bear's wives, explaining that while it might be Cheyenne custom to offer a man his spouse, he had vowed not to take another woman until he was certain that Mary's killer was dead. The explanation seemed to satisfy the two Cheyenne. Indeed, it even seemed to enhance Jubal's prestige: he was not only a mighty warrior, but also a semi-holy man living under a vow of vengeance.

As he settled down beneath the welcome warmth of a buffalo hide robe, Jubal grinned to himself as he savoured the pungent after-taste of the stew.

'I guess,' he murmured as sleep closed in, 'that some people would call it a dog's life. Still, all's well that ends well; even a dog.'

CHAPTER THREE

The camp awoke late the next morning and the pale yellow winter sun was fighting a losing battle with the grey, snow-laden sky when Jubal stuck his head out of the tepee's opening. He scooped snow from the fresh fall around the skin tent to bathe his face and was feeling more alert when Little Bear appeared in the entrance carrying a steaming tin bowl full of hot water.

'I know white men grow hair on their faces,' smiled the Indian, 'so I bring water for shaving.'

'You're pretty sharp,' Jubal replied, working up a lather of shaving soap from the small stick he carried in his saddle-bag. He proceeded to shave carefully, feeling the contours of his firm jawline as he applied the cut-throat razor. He carried a small metal mirror which he used for both shaving and, sometimes, to ascertain whether or not a patient was still breathing. When he had finished and wiped the last traces of soap from his face he pulled on his white shirt and grey vest, topped it with his shoulder holster and then donned the matching grey coat. He draped his heavy buffalo skin top-coat around his shoulders and ventured out into the waking village.

Where the night before only the men had been in evidence there were now women and children, moving about the camp on various domestic chores. The men rested easily before their tepees, calmly watching the busy women prepare the morning meal.

'I know it's not germane,' remarked Jubal as he squatted down beside Little Bear, 'but your womenfolk sure aren't liberated.'

He spent the next few minutes explaining his comment to the puzzled Indian who finally snorted in disbelief at the idea of the squaws doing anything other than tend to the

21

needs of their men.

'Men hunt and fight,' he told Jubal with total assurance, 'women cook and work. That's how it should be.'

'I'm not arguing,' Jubal grinned, wondering how some of the white women he had met would react, 'just commenting.'

They settled into a companionable silence as Little Bear's squaw brought them food from the nearby cooking fire. Jubal was careful not to ask what the dish contained, choosing simply to enjoy the tasty contents. When they had finished, Little Bear wiped his greasy fingers on his buckskin shirt while Jubal, feeling almost fastidious, washed his in snow. Then they wandered through the camp to inspect the Cheyenne pony herd. Jubal could see, now that it was daylight, why the Indians had chosen this site. Sheltered by high ridges on three sides and the treeline on the fourth, it was well-protected from the winter's snowfalls. The horse herd was penned into a bowl-like depression that even in midwinter afforded some grass and Jubal's own mount, bigger than the wiry Indian ponies, was contentedly cropping the first greenery it had seen in some time.

They were walking back towards Little Bear's lodge when three Indians cantered into the village. They came to an abrupt halt before the tepee Jubal knew belonged to the Cheyenne chief, Big Wolf, and dismounted. Eager boys ran forward to take the newcomers' ponies and they disappeared into the tent.

'Sioux,' grunted Little Bear, 'they camp north of here. They must have come for a council.'

He seemed worried and Jubal pressed, as casually as he could, for more information. For some reason the Indian had grown uneasy. He ignored Jubal's questions, steering the talk away from the strangers' visit and Jubal thought that he appeared almost embarrassed by the presence of a white man in camp.

As they drew level with the brightly decorated tepee of the chief, Big Wolf appeared at the entrance and called to Little Bear. The Indian hurried over, leaving Jubal to stroll back through the village. There was a tangible air of expectancy in the camp and the silent glances that followed Jubal's passage back to Little Bear's lodge prompted him to casually loosen the Colt in its shoulder holster. The atmosphere had changed with dramatic suddenness: earlier, Jubal had felt completely at ease; now he sensed a threat.

There was little, however, that he could do single-handed against a whole village. So he chose to wait calmly and see what would happen. He strolled casually past Little Bear's tepee and entered his own tent. Turning his back to the entrance he pulled the Spencer from its protecting blanket and quickly checked the load. He levered a shell into the breech, then eased the hammer down before laying the rifle on a blanket just inside the entrance. If anything happened he could reach it swiftly and get off at least one shot. He hunkered down outside the tent to await events.

They were not long in coming.

Big Wolf, a worried-looking Little Bear and the three Sioux emerged from the chief's tent and headed over towards Jubal. Like the Cheyenne, the Sioux braves were dressed in buckskin shirts and leggings with blankets draped over their shoulders. All three wore eagle feathers in their long, black hair and carried tomahawks. Unlike the Cheyenne, they wore paint on their faces. Long bands of black bisected their broad noses, running from cheekbone to cheekbone, and beneath the black band ran another bright red line.

They came to a halt in front of Jubal and Little Bear translated for his chief.

'Our brothers of the Sioux want to know what a white man is doing in a Cheyenne camp. We have told them of your fight with the buffalo men, but they say you are a white-eyes' spy. We have told them that we do not believe this to be true, but they say they want to question you.'

'Guess everyone's got a right to his own opinions,' Jubal remarked mildly. He rose to his feet, his small stature forcing him to look up at the tall Indians. 'Tell them to go ahead.'

A burst of guttural language followed Little Bear's translation.

'They say: what is a white man doing in the land of the Indians?'

'Just passing through,' replied Jubal, 'heading for St. Louis.'

'They say: are you not like the others who come to steal our buffalo and hunt for the yellow metal you call gold?'

'No,' Jubal answered, 'I'm not like the others. I've killed some of the others because I saved you.'

'They say: you must be a spy sent to find our camps.'

Jubal sighed wearily. It did not seem to matter what colour a man's skin was, there were some people who just did not believe what they were told.

'Tell them,' he said, 'that I am a doctor not a scout. I couldn't find your camps if I wanted to and if I did,' he looked around at the now-silent village, 'I reckon you could move it before I had a chance to tell anybody.'

He listened as Little Bear translated, watching the faces of the Sioux. It was hard to decipher any expression on those broad, impassive dials, but the grunt that burst from the lips of the tallest Indian was unmistakable: he did not believe the story.

'They repeat,' said Little Bear, 'that you must be a spy. Otherwise you would not be here.'

'Maybe I fell from the sky,' retorted Jubal, addressing his comment to the leading Sioux. 'You too could be a spy.'

Little Bear looked distinctly nervous at this outburst, but translated it none the less.

The angry torrent of words that followed made it clear to Jubal that his attack had gone home.

'They say that you are a liar and a spy,' said Little Bear, distress showing in his eyes, 'and that you must fight to prove the truth of your words.'

Jubal grinned tightly. 'Any time,' he barked, wondering if it might not be better to just ride away and take his chances with an arrow in the back.

Little Bear passed on his acceptance of the challenge and for the first time emotion showed itself on the face of the tallest Sioux. A wolfish smile spread across his face and his black eyes shone with anticipation. Jubal noticed for the first time that he was carrying a brightly painted stick beneath his blanket. Now it was brandished in Jubal's face so that the long hanks of hair tied down its length danced in the cold air. Jubal saw that most of them were fair, ranging from

24

dark brown to blonde: the kind of hair no Indian would grow.

Big Wolf and the three Sioux turned on their heels and left Jubal standing with Little Bear. The Indian gestured that they should sit down. After they had settled themselves on Jubal's spread blanket Little Bear began to explain the ritual of the coming combat. It seemed that the Sioux had suffered badly from the ravages of the buffalo hunters and the encroachment of gold miners into the Black Hills area. These mountains were held sacred by both tribes and they had fought a number of skirmishes in their attempts to deter the whites from trespassing. The result had been a string of new forts and regular campaigns by the Army to persuade the 'hostiles' that they should give up what was theirs in the face of the white men's gold-hunger.

Now the Sioux were gathering their scattered lodges in the largest winter camp they had ever formed. In the spring they intended to mount an all-out campaign against the invading whites. The three braves had been sent to Big Wolf's village to warn the Cheyenne of the coming fight and ask them to join their red brothers.

The Cheyenne, however, were wary of challenging the might of the American Army and both Little Bear and his chief hoped that there might be a chance to talk with the white authorities before rushing headlong into battle. This, allied to their natural friendliness and more liberal viewpoint, had prompted them to accept Jubal into the village. They hoped that by proving their good intentions they might persuade him to carry a message to the authorities. The Sioux, on the other hand, were all set for war and – not without reason – regarded any white man as a potential enemy. The three messengers were especially vocal in their denunciations and firmly believed that an alliance of the Sioux tribes and the Cheyenne could drive the whites from the Black Hills and the surrounding territory. Elk, the warrior who had challenged Jubal, was next to Sitting Bull and Crazy Horse in his hatred of all white men. And he was a mighty warrior, famous for his skill in battle. It was obvious that Little Bear was seriously concerned for his friend.

25

'I've been in fights before,' Jubal remarked, 'and I'm still alive to talk about them.'

'But you have never fought Elk,' countered Little Bear. 'He has taken many scalps in battle and killed three men in hand-to-hand combat.'

'I've never taken scalps or a tally,' Jubal said, 'but I've killed a few myself.'

'The white man's way,' answered the Indian. 'When you fight Elk, you will fight his way.'

'I guess that when a man has to fight, he has to fight: there's some things he can't talk his way around.'

'But Jubal,' Little Bear pronounced the name Indian-style so that it came out as Joob-al, 'you will fight with knives and tomahawks inside the circle of fire.'

Jubal grinned mirthlessly. 'I've been in hotter spots.'

CHAPTER FOUR

The fight was to take place that evening, after the tribe's hunting party had returned, so that everyone could watch the combat. Little Bear had explained that victory would establish the winner as the one in the right: whoever dealt the fatal blow would have been guided by the Great Spirit. It was, Jubal thought as he sat alone in his tepee, not unlike the mortal combats he had read about back in England, when two armoured men would hack at one another until only one remained on his feet. The only essential difference was that both he and Elk would be half-naked. And, he reminded himself, he had a wound in his side that could open all too easily.

With that thought in mind he applied himself to a careful personal examination. He unwrapped the bandage around his side and studied the bullet wound. It was healing nicely, but he administered fresh iodine and salve before wadding more lint over the scars and binding a fresh bandage tight around his ribs. Then he pulled a small bottle and a hypodermic syringe from his medical bag, punctured the seal on the bottle after washing the tip of the syringe's needle in boiling water, and injected himself with the colourless fluid. It was a mild compound of morphine that would kill most of the pain he was likely to feel if the wound should open up. And, he thought, a good deal of the pain from any cuts he might receive. It felt almost like cheating, but all was fair in love and war and Elk would be coated in bear grease to make his body slippery should Jubal grab him.

Jubal himself had rejected Little Bear's suggestion that he, too, should coat his body with the smelly, oily fat. It could be an advantage, but he preferred to rely on his speed and strength and he was chary of the effect semi-rancid fat might have on an open wound.

He finished his preparations as dusk was falling and, his topcoat hung around his bare shoulders, pushed aside the tent flap and stepped outside. Little Bear was waiting for him, carrying a tomahawk and a wicked-bladed Bowie knife, the long, curved edge glinting dangerously in the light from the numerous fires. Towards the centre of the village, where a ring of tents provided a natural arena, a circle of fires had been built. Their flames licked high up into the evening air, sending darting shadows from the surrounding tepees and lighting the faces of the Cheyenne with demonic colour.

Elk was standing silently to one side of the fire-ring, flanked by his two companions. A scarlet and blue blanket was draped around his glistening shoulders and Jubal noticed that he was well-muscled with the kind of hard, solid structure that came from handling horses and weapons.

Jubal himself gave the gathered Indians something of a surprise as he approached the centre of the village. Although he was only about five feet six inches tall and, consequently, rather shorter than most of the Indians, his slender body was well-muscled and large-boned. He knew that fully dressed he appeared rather insignificant and had been counting on that misleading aspect to make Elk overconfident. He was sure of his own strength, which greatly outstripped his outward appearance and figured that even though the Sioux stood a good three inches taller, he would have a fair chance of winning.

Little Bear took his topcoat and indicated that Jubal should step forwards to where Satanka stood intoning a prayer. Elk had already handed his blanket to one of his companions and now faced the medicine man with knife and hatchet clasped firmly before him. Jubal followed suit and stood silent as Satanka waved a rattle and a feathered stick over his head. Then Elk turned and darted between two fires that were slightly wider apart than the others. Jubal jumped into the burning ring of fire and the flames grew higher as the Cheyenne piled more dried branches on.

In the centre of the circle the light was intense, the ring of flames compensating for the waning illumination of the day. Jubal and Elk were starkly outlined as they crouched facing one another.

They paced warily around the ring, each man dropping into the instinctive crouch of a knife fighter as he eyed his opponent's face. Then Elk sprang forwards, a shrill war-cry ringing from his lips. Jubal poised on the balls of his feet as the Indian's tomahawk swung in a flat, vicious arc towards his skull. At the last moment he ducked, swinging his body sideways so that the hatchet whistled over his head. At the same time he brought his knife around to block Elk's thrust and swung his own tomahawk at the Sioux's belly. Elk twisted and weaved his body around Jubal's blow, cutting savagely with his knife at the white man's face.

Jubal sprang back, causing the Indian to fall off-balance for a moment. He used the time to power himself forwards, hacking down with the tomahawk as he simultaneously swung the Bowie knife upwards.

Elk smashed the knife aside with the flat of his axe and turned sideways on to the down-coming blow. He used his knife to parry the hatchet, but even so the sharp edge ripped a strip of skin from his forearm. The watching Indians gasped at the sight of Jubal taking the first blood. And Elk himself grunted in reluctant admiration.

'White man fight good for squaw killer,' he grunted, revealing for the first time that he spoke some English.

'Good enough for the likes of you,' answered Jubal.

'Nobody like me,' Elk replied.

'I'm not surprised,' Jubal grinned as he deflected a blow aimed at his head.

They broke apart and circled again, each man looking for an opening. Elk saw it first and came in fast, his hatchet weaving a glittering pattern of light before Jubal's face. The white man backed up until he felt the fires on his back, then hurled himself to one side as the Indian's knife swung in beneath the axe. Jubal was not quite fast enough and the knife cut a ragged slash across his ribs. He felt warm blood oozing down his side to clot in the bandage but had no time to register any pain as he avoided the tomahawk blow that followed.

He ducked under the blow, using the Indian's greater

size against him, and lifted his own axe upwards in a curving swing.

The blunt back connected with the Sioux warrior's chin, snapping his mouth shut over the fragments of broken teeth that glittered white on his lips. Jubal rolled to one side as his opponent spat blood and bone on to the hard-packed earth and brought his knife around in a side slash that would have severed Jubal's neck had he remained where he was. As Jubal rolled, Elk threw himself forwards, his hatchet swinging at Jubal's legs. The smaller man felt a stab of pain as the heavy weapon crashed off his right leg, spattering blood into the surrounding fires. But the blow failed to smash his legs as Elk had intended and the Indian's momentum carried him straight on to Jubal's opuththrust feet. The smaller man straightened his legs, lifting the Sioux up over his head and sending him flying through the air.

As he crashed down Jubal regained his feet and leaped forwards. His knife flashed down, but Elk rolled over so that the blade dug deep into the soil. As the shock of the contact ran the length of Jubal's arm, the Indian flailed his tomahawk at the white man. Jubal bent his elbow, letting the knife go rather than risk a shattered arm. The blow drew blood from the inside of his elbow without severing any of the vital tendons there and Jubal pushed himself away. Both men sprang to their feet, panting with the exertion. Blood dripped from Elk's smashed mouth and the wound in his left arm. Jubal's ribs and elbow bled from the cuts he had received and he eyed his fallen knife longingly.

The Sioux followed his gaze and with a gleeful whoop kicked the knife into the nearest fire. Then he screamed and charged straight at Jubal. The smaller man swung his tomahawk in a defensive circle that connected violently with the Indian's own blade. Elk howled as the shock of the blow numbed his hand, but his knife curved in to slash a second cut across Jubal's ribs.

Jubal gasped and reversed the swing of his axe so that it whistled in between Elk's momentarily outflung arms. The Indian saw the blow coming and sucked in his stomach, curving his spine backwards in an attempt to avoid it. But Jubal

30

was too fast: the tomahawk drove into Elk's ribs on the left side. Jubal felt the flesh give way under the blow and saw a vivid red wound open in the Indian's side like the obscenely painted lips of some gaping fish. Ribs splintered under the impact and Elk was knocked off his feet.

It was the kind of blow that would have smashed most men into unconsciousness, but Elk's insane hatred over-rode the messages of pain driving into his brain. He came up on his feet, his teeth parted in a savage, animal-like snarl, and hurled himself on.

Jubal side-stepped as the tomahawk went past his head and smashed his leg across the Indian's. The Sioux was lifted off his feet and crashed full-length on to the ground.

Jubal spun around and brought his hatchet down in a murderous arc. But again Elk's skill in combat saved him. He rolled aside, kicking upwards as he turned so that one foot pushed Jubal's hand aside while the other crashed into the white man's cheek. Jubal felt his mouth fill with blood from an internal cut as his forward movement caused him to fall towards the Indian's body. He spat a stream of bloody spittle into the Sioux's face as he twisted his midriff aside. The un-expected action served to put Elk off his stroke and the knife that was lifting towards Jubal's belly went harmlessly past.

The Indian was seriously weakened now by the flow of blood from his gashed side and he knew that he must end the fight soon or die in the circle of flames.

Jubal was equally aware of his own deteriorating condition. The morphine he had injected was killing most of the pain from his wounds and, anyway, they were less serious than his opponent's. But even so, he had felt the bullet hole in his side open up and knew that he risked internal bleeding if he went on much longer.

Elk was back on his feet, his hate-clouded eyes following Jubal as the white man moved towards him.

'You a better fighter than I thought,' he snarled.

'Guess both our knives cut two ways,' replied Jubal.

'You don't have a knife,' gasped the Sioux as he hurled himself forwards.

'So my iron's in the fire,' Jubal grunted, meeting Elk's

charge halfway, 'one tomahawk's enough to cut down a wooden Indian.'

He parried the man's knife with the hatchet as his left hand grasped the Indian's wrist. It was enough to slow the swinging hatchet, but his fingers slid off the heavily greased limb so that the weapon continued its downwards trajectory before he could step back to avoid it. The blade cut a long, crimson path down his chest, carving a bloody gash from shoulder to waist and splashing Elk with bright, red blood.

The Indian whooped in triumph and drove the head of his axe hard into Jubal's groin.

Jubal screamed as raw pain flooded through his body, a wave of agony washing over the protective effects of the morphine. He doubled around the blow, using his free hand to push himself away from Elk before the Sioux could use his knife. Jubal's knees were drawn up in a protecting ball as he fell backwards, so that he rolled over to the very edge of the fire-circle. He could feel the flames licking across his back as he came to a stop and forced himself to ignore the pain as he straightened his legs.

He saw Elk darting straight at him, hatchet lifted for a killing blow as the knife swung low to guard against attack. Mindlessly, Jubal's hand thrust into the flames to grasp a brand.

He ignored the pain as he powered himself up directly into the path of the warrior's charge. The flaming brand curved upwards at Elk's face and the Sioux instinctively brought his arms around to protect himself. Jubal thrust the torch straight into his eyes and smelled burning hair mingle with the sweet odour of scorched flesh as the Indian screamed and clutched at his hideously blistered cheeks.

He had dropped his weapons in his sudden panic and Jubal seized the advantage. He swung his own tomahawk in a great over-hand blow that smashed the blade down on to Elk's unprotected skull. He felt the cranium collapse under the force of the attack and saw the Indian's head split, literally, in two as the blade cut down through bone and muscle.

A great splash of grey-white brain matter fell soggily over Elk's shoulders and Jubal's own face, followed by a spout of

crimson that sizzled in the nearby fire. Jubal let go the tomahawk and stepped back as Elk stood there. The axe protruded
like an extended nose from his shattered head as his eyes, now
farther apart than ever before, stared blankly into the flames.
His upper lip hung in two sections as the lower dripped blood
down his chest.

He took a step forwards as his dead lungs expelled the last
air they would ever need in a long, gargling moan that spewed
blood out around the two strips of his severed tongue, then
he pitched forwards into the flames.

Jubal gagged as the stench of roasting flesh choked his
nostrils and stepped groggily back from the ruined body of
his assailant.

He was still clammy from the hideous mess of blood and
brains when the Cheyenne jumped, whooping, into the ring
of fire. Satanka and Big Wolf hushed the Indians silent as
Little Bear hurried to Jubal's side. Big Wolf began to speak,
the Indians quieting as his deep voice echoed around the
camp.

'He says,' Little Bear explained, 'that the Great Spirit
guided your hand. Therefore you were right. Elk spoke with
a forked tongue and you showed it to us.'

'I guess I did,' Jubal muttered, 'but not the way you
mean it.'

CHAPTER FIVE

Jubal spent the next few days recovering from the combined effects of his re-opened bullet wound and those he had incurred fighting Elk. The dead Indian's two companions departed the morning after the fight for the Sioux encampments strung out between Denver and the Little Big Horn river. They carried with them Big Wolf's demand that no action be taken until he had had a chance to speak with Jubal and try to persuade the small white man to carry a message to the authorities.

The Sioux had reluctantly agreed, promising that they would inform their war chiefs of the unexpected result of the trial by combat and the Cheyenne's desire to maintain peace if it should prove possible.

Jubal lay in a feverish state, alternating between periods of lucidity and rambling, half-conscious delirium. Before passing out he had taken needles and suture thread from his black valise and carefully – if painfully – sown the wounds crisscrossing his ribs closed. They would leave ugly scars, but once he had cleaned and closed them he did not anticipate any secondary infections. The bullet wound was painful but not serious and he hoped that a fresh bandage and a period of rest would cure it completely. Satanka had taken the opportunity to demonstrate his friendship and feeling as a fellow-healer by taking over the supervision of Jubal's convalescence. On several occasions Jubal emerged from a spell of fever-ridden sleep to discover the shaman carefully dressing his wounds with a combination of his own herbal remedies and bandages from Jubal's bag.

When he finally recovered full consciousness the first sight to greet his eyes was the grinning faces of Satanka and Little Bear. They called for food as Jubal struggled into his clothes after examining his wounds. They were all clean and

34

showed no sign of infection; he felt weak, but that was only to be expected and nothing that a few days' more rest and a reasonable diet could not cure. For a week longer he took things easy, lying outside his tepee as Little Bear's wife brought him food, talking with the Cheyenne who now flocked to speak to him through the translations of his two friends.

At last, when he was fully recovered, Big Wolf approached. The chief wanted Jubal to ride into Denver and contact the authorities. He hoped that a white man might succeed where Indians had failed in persuading the powers-that-be of the good intentions of the Cheyenne and the indignities they had suffered at the hands of the white people.

Jubal agreed. He had been heading for Denver anyway so it was no hardship to continue his journey. Especially as Big Wolf offered him two saddlebags filled with the yellow metal that was drawing miners like flies to the honey-pot of the Black Hills. Jubal had little knowledge of gold-mining but still estimated that the two bags contained something in the region of a thousand dollars' worth of gold: enough to ensure Andy Prescott's fees for several months. So he waited until the last of the mid-winter blizzards had cleared and set out.

The foothills of the Rockies were still covered with snow that blanketed the great open spaces with blinding white, broken only by the stark black trunks of the great fir trees rearing up through the drifts. He was accompanied as far as the frozen banks of the South Platte River by a group of seven warriors led by Little Bear. They left him by the river with a packhorse loaded with supplies and instructions to follow the river south into Denver.

Jubal promised again to carry their message to the authorities and return himself, if he could, with the answer. Otherwise he would endeavour to get a message through by some other means.

Little Bear assured Jubal that he would be welcome in the Cheyenne territory at any time and, clearly sorry to see his friend depart alone, turned his pony west and rode off through the snow. Jubal turned his own mount south and led the packhorse behind him down the edge of the river. He rode for two days without seeing any sign of another being alive in the bleak, winter-crusted landscape. His only companions were the two horses, their nostrils spuming jets of steam into the freezing air as they ploughed slowly on through the deep snowdrifts. The going was arduous and Jubal was forced to make frequent detours whenever the snow became too deep to negotiate. He had only the river and the pale sun to steer by and was required to make fairly frequent side-trips to find the South Platte whenever he was pushed away from it by deep snow. He realized that he could get easily lost in the snowfields of the High Plains country and drift aimlessly until his food ran out if he did not keep the river on his left, so he stayed close even though it meant he would probably take longer to reach Denver.

His first sight of the town came on the third day. Columns of wispy smoke stood straight up above the plain and the deep snow began to recede under the impact of numerous wagon tracks. Jubal rode on, relishing the thought of a hot bath and a soft bed. And, more than anything else, the taste of a cheroot.

He pushed on through the steadily clearing snow until he drew level with the town. Like most western settlements it was a ragged sprawl of wooden buildings, few reaching higher than a single storey although four or five boasted a third level and about a dozen of the structures reached two floors. It was the first town of any size Jubal had seen since leaving Laredo and the biggest gathering of buildings since St. Louis. Standing up squat and smoky out of the bare white plain it looked like an ugly jumble of children's building blocks dropped carelessly on to a clean white cloth.

But the aspect of white civilization carried little concern for Jubal at that moment. His more immediate problem was getting across the river. The South Platte was running too fast at this point for any reliable thickness of surface ice to form and Jubal was wary of trusting the pack-ice crusting the surface of the river. On the far bank he spotted the low outline of a ferry and yelled across. A figure, bulky in winter clothing emerged from a small hut beside the landing stage and began to haul the floating platform through the water by means of a long rope secured to either bank and connected to the ferry by a winch-wheel. As the rough boat drew closer Jubal could hear muttered curses floating across the frozen water. He sat his horse silently, waiting for the grumbling ferryman to bring his craft in to the western bank. When it grounded Jubal heeled his mount forwards on to the creaking boards.

'Afore you come aboard, mister,' the ferryman rasped, 'I'd like to see the colour o' yore money.'

'So what's the tariff?' demanded Jubal, irritated by his first brush with civilization since leaving the Cheyenne.

'Five cents a head, eight for horses,' answered the man, puffing a gust of evil-smelling pipe smoke in Jubal's direction, 'with the exception of pack animals. They cost ten cents.' He paused to make a mental calculation with obvious effort. 'That makes it twenty-three cents in all.'

Jubal pulled a silver dollar from an inside pocket of his coat and threw it to the ferryman.

He watched as the grinning face ducked to test the coin with blackened teeth before a grimy hand delved into a pocket to produce, reluctantly, the required change.

'What's your name,' he asked. 'Shylock?'

'Nossir,' the man answered as Jubal led his horses on board, 'it's Brian. You ask anyone for Brian up on the levee. They all know me.'

Jubal chose not to answer and the ferry pulled silently out into the stream. As it moved towards the far bank he saw that most of the buildings along the river front were low structures equipped with loading bays and winching gear. He guessed that they were warehouses for the buffalo skins brought in by hunters. The hides were most likely cured and stored there until a boat appeared to take them along the Platte to its junction with the Missouri. That would be cheaper than shipping the skins out on the rail line heading East. It would also account, he thought as they approached the other bank, for the vile stink that filled the air.

During his stay with the Cheyenne, Jubal had grown accustomed to the smell of animal fat and half-cured hides. After the first few days it had become a natural part of the village's life, but this was different. He had got an inkling when he first rode up to the buffalo hunters' camp, but this surpassed anything he had smelled on the unwashed bodies of the men he had left back in the high snow country. It was a raw, rotting odour that hit his nose with almost physical force, causing the horses to stir restively. How many dead buffalo went to make up such a stench Jubal could not imagine, but he was grateful that the wind appeared to blow from the east so that the smell was carried out across the river, rather than back into the town.

He hurried off the ferry and pushed both horses into a fast trot to carry them clear of the stinking riverside district. He headed down a wide road that promised to lead into the centre of Denver and was glad when the stink faded behind him. He slowed to a walk, eyeing the low, wooden buildings to either side. Back of the warehouses stood a number of decrepit-looking tenement buildings boasting cheap prices for single rooms and meals and even cheaper prices for drinks. Beyond them lay more respectable houses and then numerous stores and office buildings. Jubal went on until he reached the main thoroughfare, a wide, rutted street flanked by saloons, more stores and several brightly lit cathouses. Here and there a hotel or stable stood out, but he decided to make his money last and look for somewhere cheaper. He reined in outside a saloon and dismounted, leaving both horses at the hitching post.

Inside, the place was like most American saloons west of the Mississippi: wooden floored, smoky and rowdy. A long bar stretched the length of one wall and the central area was dotted with tables, chairs and drinking men. Saloon girls in garish dresses and even more vivid make-up moved among the tables, the lurid feathers decorating their piled-up hair bobbing fitfully in the blue-grey air.

One of them approached Jubal as he paused just inside the swing doors.

'Buy a girl a drink, mister?'

'I'd be delighted, ma'am,' he replied, exposing his broken front teeth in a boyishly charming grin, 'but you're hardly a girl and I'm only here for the drink.'

'Fuck you!' snarled the spurned whore, showing Jubal a set of blackened dentures.

'Not if I can help it, ma'am,' he smiled stepping away from her in the direction of the bar.

As he leant his elbows on the polished surface he became aware of a smell that rose above the odour of tobacco and alcohol: the smell he had noticed riding into the town. He glanced around the hazy room at the men drinking there and saw that most were clad in battered pants and sweat-stained cotton shirts. A few sported faded buckskins and, occasionally, a buffalo hide coat. He caught the attention of an over-worked barkeep and asked the origin of the stench.

'Fer Chrissakes, friend,' the barman looked around almost furtively, as though afraid of someone overhearing Jubal's words. 'Keep yore voice down. If there's one thing a buffalo hunter don't want to hear it's the fact that he stinks.'

He looked around again and beckoned Jubal to lean closer across the bar. 'Even if it's a pure fact that he does.'

Jubal grinned. He had smelled worse odours and he did not want to precipitate a fight with anyone if he could help it – even a malodorous skin hunter.

'All right,' he said, 'I'll keep my voice down in return for some information and a drink. I need a stable and a place to bed down.'

The bartender breathed a sigh of relief as the prospect of a potentially expensive fight faded away and pushed a glass accompanied by a whiskey bottle in Jubal's direction.

'You got a deal, friend. The south side's the expensive section.'

'Forget it,' said Jubal, 'what I'm looking for is a few dollars less than expensive.'

'Well,' the barman was polishing glasses in a momentary lull, 'north side's real cheap and the river's cheaper. If you can stand the smell. But if you want some place decent and reasonably clean then Lizzie's is your best bet.'

'How do I find it?' Jubal asked.

'Head south 'bout fifty paces an' you'll see a roadway marked Abbot's Lane, go down it eighty-odd paces an' you're at Lizzie's. She's always got time for strangers.'

'Thanks.' Jubal sipped his drink slowly; he was not a great drinker and had been without liquor for long enough to be careful of the amount he consumed. 'How about the stable?'

'Next door. Run by Lizzie's husband. He's called Larry. Quirky kind of a guy, but OK if you don't mind someone who keeps quotin' what he calls literature.'

Jubal tossed a coin on to the bar and up-ended his glass before the man could refill it.

'Grateful for the information.' He touched the brim of his grey derby and turned towards the door. Outside, he untied the two horses, climbed into the saddle and headed down the street looking for the place the barman had suggested. It was closer than he had thought and a few moments' riding brought him level with the entrance. He turned off the main drag and walked his mount up the side alley until he spotted a sign informing passers-by that Lizzie's boarding-house and stable welcomed all guests. He dismounted and went inside.

A young woman with long brown hair greeted him enthusiastically.

'Hi, stranger. I'm Lizzie. You lookin' for a room?'

Jubal grinned. The place was clean and free of the buffalo stink.

'Yes, ma'am,' he doffed his derby in greeting, 'I need a room for a few days. And I could use a bath.'

'We can offer both,' Lizzie smiled back, 'and if you want a stable then there's one right next door. My husband's there now.'

Jubal put down a five dollar deposit that guaranteed him a room, a bath and two meals a day for the next week and headed for the stable. He was met at the door by a young man sporting shoulder-length black hair and a pair of grubby, work-stained levis. Gold spectacles decorated his face and it occurred to Jubal that he would have looked more at home in a printing office than a stable.

'Hark, what news from distant lands?' he greeted Jubal.

'I guess I wouldn't know,' Jubal replied, handing over the reins of the two horses. 'I just rode in.'

'Sad, sad,' muttered the unlikely stable man. 'Much ado about nothing seems the order of the day in Denver. I should have stayed in Connecticut. I come from Hartford,' he added.

'Sounds like you should be a writer or something,' Jubal

remarked as he slid his saddlebags clear of the horse's back.

'I tried,' said Larry, 'but all people read nowadays are cheap dime novels. So we came West.'

He shrugged theatrically as he led the horses to handy stalls and began to rub them down.

Jubal left him working and returned to the rooming house. Lizzie showed him to a small, but scrupulously clean, room with the promise of a hot bath in a few minutes. Jubal dumped his gear in a corner, resting the Spencer against the wall beside the bed and then, with a sigh of relief, stretched out atop the sheets. He was not there long before Lizzie's shout announced that his bath was ready and he headed gratefully in the direction of the steam-filled room indicated by the proprietress.

He soaked himself until the water began to cool, then towelled himself dry and returned to his room. He took a fresh white shirt from his saddlebag and knotted his black string tie around his neck before pulling on the grey English-cut suit. The Colt was fully loaded and Jubal slid the gun into his shoulder holster, dropping a handful of cartridges into a coat pocket. Lizzie gave him directions to the nearest barber shop and Jubal promised to return later for the evening meal which was thrown in with the price of the room.

In the barber shop Jubal ordered a shave and haircut. As the barber began to crop his thick black hair to its customary closeness, Jubal questioned him about the town. As he had expected, the man was a useful source of information: like the saloons, barber shops were as much social meeting-places as they were business establishments. Jubal learned that Denver was currently filled with buffalo hunters waiting out the lean winter months. The bulk of the hunting was done during the spring and summer, when the herds were fat and plentiful. Then the hunters slaughtered vast numbers of the big animals, bringing the hides into Denver by the wagon load. During the cold period when the buffalo were thin and the plains swept by blizzards the hunters gathered in Denver to spend the money gotten earlier in the year. A few groups – such as the one Jubal had encountered – stayed out late, but most of the hunters wintered in town. It was a powder keg

41

situation as large bands of men with money in their pockets grew increasingly bored with their enforced inactivity. Sudden, violent fights were frequent and the town marshal was often called out to dampen a situation that might flare into gunplay.

'How about the Army?' Jubal asked. 'Do they have anyone in town?'

'Sure,' the barber answered, 'there's a detachment of cavalry camped out by the river. Been there since the start of the injun trouble.'

He was working on the nape of Jubal's neck, so the next question was muffled.

'Who's in command?'

'A captain called Simms. Young guy, but he seems to know what he's doin'. Leastways, we ain't had any injun trouble for a while.'

Jubal thanked the man for the information and paid for the shave and haircut. He stepped out on to the boardwalk and, after eyeing the churned-up slush that constituted the street, decided to get his horse for the short journey to the Army camp.

Larry had just finished grooming the animal when Jubal reappeared in the stable and he was clearly upset by the decision to take the freshly curried and combed animal out into the muddy streets. Jubal, however, overrode his objections and to the accompaniment of Larry's grumbling saddled up and mounted. He walked the horse out of the stable and headed towards the main thoroughfare. The barber's directions took him straight to the Army camp that lay to the northern end of the town, beyond the warehouse district and out of range of the all-pervading stench of drying buffalo hides.

The bivouac stretched over a considerable area, an orderly array of white and khaki tents pitched in straight lines. Guidons fluttered in the evening breeze and Jubal could see soldiers moving purposefully about the encampment. At the centre stood a wooden building, fronted by a tall, white-painted flagpole that carried the Stars and Stripes at its top. Below the American flag hung the divisional pennant of the 7th

Cavalry. Jubal rode slowly between the rows of tents, armed troopers patrolled the perimeter of the bivouac but they had allowed Jubal through without question. Now he headed straight for the hut that appeared to be the nerve centre of the camp.

He reined in before the building and dismounted as the two soldiers on guard brought their carbines to the ready position.

'Halt!' came the Army's traditional greeting. 'State yore business.'

'I'd like to see Captain Simms,' Jubal said easily, hitching his mount to the rail of the building's porch. 'Got some business I want to discuss.'

'OK, mister,' the older of the two guards grunted, 'wait there while I see if'n he wants to talk to you.'

He knocked on the door and then stuck his head inside.

'Civilian out here, sir,' he announced, 'says he's got business with you.'

The reply must have been affirmative because Jubal was ushered inside and the door pulled shut behind him. On the far side of the small room, behind a plain wooden desk littered with papers, sat a man of about Jubal's age. Shoulder-length brown hair grew down over the epaulettes of his blue uniform jacket and a neatly trimmed beard made him look somewhat older than he apparently was. He smiled as Jubal entered the room and stood up.

'I'm Simms,' he said. 'What can I do for you?'

'If you're in command here you can do quite a lot,' Jubal replied.

'I think you'd better explain,' said the young captain, 'but before you do I may as well tell you that we already have all the civilian contracts we need. And you don't look like a scout.'

Jubal smiled. 'I'm not and I don't want to sell you anything either. I'm here to give you some information.'

Simms looked doubtful. It was obvious to Jubal that he was frequently pestered by civilians seeking to grease their way into a lucrative Army contract whereby they could supply inferior goods at inflated prices. He sat down, ignoring the soldier's frown of disapproval.

43

'You're here to stop a war between the Indians and the whites; right?'

The captain looked more interested now.

'I am here to contain the hostiles,' he agreed, 'and to ensure that Americans may travel in safety.'

'Hell,' Jubal cut him off before he could go any farther, 'you're here to hold the lid down on a powder keg that's already smouldering.'

Captain Simms stared at his outspoken visitor, unsure of his reply. Army doctrine and personal honesty fought visibly as he decided how to answer. After a few moments he decided.

'It's not the official statement,' he grinned, coming to a decision, 'but yes: that's about it.'

Jubal relaxed: now that the young soldier had demonstrated his willingness to speak frankly, the message would be easier to deliver.

'All right,' he said, 'so you know the Indians are ready to fight.'

'More than ready,' interjected Simms, 'they've already killed several parties of hunters and prospectors. Only a week or so ago four buffalo hunters were shot dead.'

'How do you know?' Jubal asked.

'A patrol found the bodies a few miles from their camp. Three had been killed by gun shots and one with arrows.'

Jubal chose to remain silent. He had no wish to confess himself the killer, although he felt no remorse: it would simply complicate matters.

'They were shooting buffalo on Indian land,' he said, 'if the Sioux and Cheyenne see the buffalo wiped out and their lands taken what do you expect them to do?'

'I'm a soldier, mister ...' Simms paused. 'I didn't get your name. Or why you're here.'

'Cade,' said Jubal, 'Jubal Cade. I'm a doctor.'

'We already have a medical officer,' Simms remarked stiffly, 'and if you're a Quaker or Mormon come to tell me I shouldn't be fighting the redskins you'll be wasting your time. And mine: I have orders.'

'I'm not and I didn't,' Jubal said gently, 'I just brought you a message. From Big Wolf.'

The soldier came to immediate attention, his whole body stiffening at the mention of the Cheyenne chief's name.

'Big Wolf?' he barked. 'What message?'

Jubal wondered how he should phrase his reply. He had no wish to be branded as an untrustworthy Indian lover, but was equally determined to fulfil his promise to the Cheyenne.

'I was hurt,' he began, 'the Cheyenne picked me up and saved my life. Big Wolf asked me to deliver a message. He wants to talk peace.'

'My information is that Big Wolf and his people are moving north to join the Sioux in the Powder River country,' Simms said eyeing Jubal with new interest. 'There's a big winter camp forming there. And too many bucks talking war.'

'Big Wolf,' said Jubal, 'doesn't want war. He asked me to tell you that. He wants to talk peace.'

Captain Simms looked sceptical but none the less listened as Jubal explained the Cheyenne's desire to find a solution to the threat of all-out war.

'I don't see how we can stop the buffalo hunters,' the soldier murmured, clearly attracted by the idea of organizing a solution to the problem, 'but there's already talk of the Army patrolling the Black Hills to prevent the miners from going in there.'

'So why not speak with Big Wolf?' asked Jubal, dangling the carrot of personal credit in front of the soldier. 'If you could talk him into a peace treaty you'd be a mighty important man.'

'Yes,' Simms agreed, 'but how could I meet him? If he came here, the townspeople would shoot him down. And I don't know how I could reach his camp without scaring the whole band off.'

'Maybe I can help,' Jubal remarked.

He spent the next hour explaining to the Army officer how he had first made contact with the Cheyenne, although he was careful to omit any mention of his fight with the buffalo hunters, explaining their friendly attitude and mistrust of both the white men flooding into their territory and the confidence of the more warlike Sioux. All Jubal's powers of persuasion were brought into play as he led the captain towards the conclusion he sought. The soldier seemed more reasonable than most; in spite of his frontiersman image, promoted by the long hair and the beard, he was willing to discuss the possibility of a peaceful settlement with the Indians. It was dark outside when he finally nodded his agreement and reached behind his chair for a whiskey bottle and two glasses.

'A toast, doctor,' he announced pouring the pale golden liquid, 'to peace.'

Jubal raised his own glass. 'I'll buy a piece of that action,' he grinned.

CHAPTER SIX

Denver was packed with men as Jubal rode back to the rooming house, the night was raucous with the sound of shouting, tinkling pianos and occasional shots. Food, Jubal decided, was the first thing he wanted and after that, a look at the town. It had become instinctive, he realized, to study the layout of any place he was spending time in: a defensive reaction. Automatically, he had studied the configuration of streets and alleyways passed on his way into Denver, now he was noticing the pattern between the Army bivouac and mainstreet. He grinned to himself as he noted potential escape routes, then pushed his thoughts to the back of his mind as he approached Lizzie's place.

She was as good a cook as the friendly bartender had promised and the comfortable dining-room made a tranquil contrast to the bustling streets outside. Jubal was one of the last to eat and was grateful that he could sit alone with his thoughts.

Captain Simms had agreed that he should return to the Cheyenne camp alone to arrange a meeting with Big Wolf. Simms himself had promised to send an urgent message to his commanding officer, requesting that either the senior man attend the parley or grant his junior officer the right to negotiate terms. Jubal was to be included in the talks as mediator and would leave Denver in the next day or so. But first, he reminded himself, he had to deposit the gold Big Wolf had given him in a local bank and arrange for a transfer of funds to St. Louis where Andy Prescott remained in the Lenz Clinic. Jubal lit a cheroot and decided to forget the whole thing for the remainder of the evening. He would get a drink and see if he could not get into a poker game.

Touching his hat brim in farewell to Lizzie, he shrugged into his topcoat and left the dining-room. A freezing wind was blowing in off the surrounding plain, blowing the stink from the warehouses back across the river as Jubal made his way to the centre of the town. The buildings seemed to funnel the wind so that the streets were cold despite the gusts of warm, smoky air emanating from the brightly lit saloons and whorehouses. Jubal ignored the latter and allowed his nose to pick a saloon that was slightly less redolent of buffalo hide than most of the others. He pushed through the batwing doors and headed for the bar.

'What'll it be?' asked a grinning bartender. 'We got whiskey, beer an' more whiskey.'

'Whiskey,' Jubal said, pushing a coin across the bar.

He sipped at the fiery alcohol as he surveyed the room. Three card games were in session, each with a full complement of players. Most of the men seated around the room looked, from the battered clothes they wore and the smell they gave off, to be buffalo hunters. Here and there a dark blue shirt indicated an off-duty soldier spending his meagre pay on two of the three pursuits open to an army man stationed in the High Plains country. Jubal drank slowly, waiting for someone to drop out of a game.

He was on his second whiskey when a trooper threw down his hand and declared his intention of quitting. Jubal walked over to the table and gestured at the vacant chair.

'You gents mind if I sit in?'

A heavily bearded man dressed in sweat-stained shirt and leather pants looked up.

'If you got the money, stranger, you're welcome.'

A soldier pushed the empty chair back with his boot heel. 'Come right ahead, mister. Maybe you'll change my luck.'

'Thanks,' Jubal smiled, throwing his coat over the back of a nearby chair, 'what's the ante?'

'Dollar a time,' grunted one of the three buffalo hunters, 'straight poker an' the pot's as big as we make it.'

Jubal dropped a silver dollar on to the table and took the hand the soldier dealt him. He changed two cards to fill a straight that won him a ten dollar pot and went on to win the next two hands with a full house and a set of threes. Two of the buffalo hunters were obviously inexpert card players, but

48

the bearded man and the soldier were both skilled at the game and stayed level with Jubal. After an hour one of the players dropped out and his place was taken by a second soldier. As he sat down Jubal recognized him as the older of the two guards outside Captain Simms's office.

'Hey,' he remarked as Jubal dealt him cards, 'ain't you the new scout the captain took on? The feller who reckons he can bring Big Wolf in to talk.'

Jubal was conscious of the sudden silence around the table.

'Could be,' he said easily, thumbing cards from the deck.

'Hell,' grunted a buffalo hunter, 'you mean he's the injun lover we been hearin' about?'

Jubal made an attempt to keep the game going. 'We here to play cards or not?'

'Not with a damn' injun lover,' rasped the bearded man. He kicked his chair back as he stood up. 'Them murderin' savages killed friends o' mine an' anyone who sides with 'em ain't welcome around me.'

'The killing goes two ways,' Jubal remarked mildly, 'and they're not all murderers.'

The buffalo hunter snarled and hurled his glass at the table.

'Mister,' he grated through clenched teeth, 'you're a lying squaw man an' I'm gonna tear you apart.'

He was joined by his two companions as the rest of the saloon turned to study the outburst of violence with interest. It promised to alleviate the boredom of another long winter's night.

Jubal pocketed his winnings and eyed the angry hunter. The man was a good four inches taller and built like a slab of solid rock.

'I'm not looking for any trouble,' Jubal remarked quietly, 'so why not let it go?'

'Fuck you!' bellowed the big man, his right hand clawing at the butt of his Colt.

For so big a man he was surprisingly fast and the gun was swinging up even as Jubal threw himself backwards from his sitting position. His feet were planted firmly on the plank floor and he snapped his legs straight out so that the chair tipped back as the Colt boomed. The ·45 calibre slug whistled

49

close past Jubal's head as he fell back on to the floor. As he hit he sat up, his right hand leaping inside his coat to draw the gun holstered under his left arm. He had been taught gunplay by an expert and knew that sure aim was more important than rapid fire. The big man's second shot blasted splinters from the fallen chair as Jubal rolled sideways across the floor thumbing back the hammer of his own gun.

The buffalo hunter was cursing as Jubal levelled the Colt and fired from his position on the floor. The bullet hit the hunter dead centre in his chest where his shirt parted to expose a hairy mat of curly black hairs. They turned scarlet as blood spurted from the hole drilled there and his third shot crashed into the card table. Even so he was pulling back the hammer to try again when Jubal rolled to a kneeling position and fired a second time. The shot was placed as accurately as the first and a third eye appeared in the man's forehead, redder than its two whiskey-laden partners. His head flipped back as the bullet exited through his skull, spraying blood and brain matter over the nearest onlookers. He stood for a long moment staring blindly at the ceiling as blood oozed down his face. The rictus of death tightened his fingers and his gun boomed for the last time, its discharge smashing the bullet into his own foot. Then he buckled at the knees and crashed across the table, sending cards and loose coins flying like confetti around his falling body.

'Eyes down for the dead man's hand,' muttered the soldier whose comments had begun the killing.

Jubal was on his feet now, his Colt aimed at the dead man's friends who stood staring, their hands resting on their own guns, at the corpse stretched across the table. Then something prodded his back. He was turning when the bartender's voice sounded in his ear.

'No more gunplay, stranger. I got a marshal to keep happy if I want to keep open.'

He moved around to one side so that Jubal could see the sawn-off shotgun held at waist level to cover the room. Like Jubal, the two buffalo hunters realized that the vicious weapon could spread a cloud of heavy-gauge pellets across the whole saloon before anyone else had a chance to fire. Reluctantly they raised their hands from their holsters. Jubal grinned without any humour showing on his face. The skin across his cheekbones was stretched tight and his nostrils were flared above his compressed lips. He knew the look his face assumed whenever he became angry and he knew it was the kind of look that made people nervous.

'OK,' he said tightly, 'you're calling the play. What's the next move?'

'First,' said the bartender carefully, 'you put the gun down.'

Jubal complied, lowering the hammer gently and placing the Colt on the table to one side of the spreading pool of blood that was oozing from the dead man's shattered skull.

The barman gestured at the two buffalo hunters. 'You too,' he demanded, 'drop yore guns.'

When all three Colts were on the table a soldier was detailed to carry them over to the bar and more men called upon to arrange the tables in a rough circle.

'Now you can settle it,' announced the bartender, 'bare fists an' no holds barred.' He turned to the crowd of drinkers eyeing the three combatants with avid interest. 'Ten dollars on the buffler men,' he offered.

The soldier who had first welcomed Jubal to the game took up the offer. 'I'll match that,' he said, 'ten dollars on the little guy.'

Jubal felt less confident than his supporter. Although neither of his opponents was as big as their dead partner, they were both tall and well-muscled. And they looked eager to take him apart. He removed his coat and handed it to the soldier, then carefully took his gold hunter watch from the pocket of his vest and entrusted that, too, to the trooper.

'C'mon, runt,' snarled the younger of the two men, 'let's get it over with.'

Jubal's answer was to power himself forwards in a flat dive that rammed his head into the speaker's stomach. As the man doubled over Jubal stood straight, jerking his head back so that it smashed against the man's nose. Blood spurted as the bridge of the nose broke under the impact and the man spat red froth on to the floor. In the same movement Jubal pivoted on his right foot, lashing out his left in a vicious kick aimed at the

51

second man's groin.

The buffalo hunter was ready though, and his hands grasped Jubal's ankle lifting him off the floor. He cushioned his head in his arms as he crashed against the boards and drove his other foot hard into the man's belly.

'Hell, Johnny,' gasped the winded hunter, 'quit pickin' yore nose an' come help.'

Johnny complied, swinging his boot in a savage arc that ended against Jubal's belt buckle. Nausea brought tears to Jubal's eyes as the pain of the kick flooded through his system. He brought his legs up to protect his midriff and groin from another attack and rolled away from the flailing boots. The other hunter sought to stomp him and Jubal was forced to roll across the floor in an effort to escape. He came up against a chair and reached out to grab one of the legs. He lifted it across his body in a swinging blow that connected with the legs of his opponent. Tangled, the man fell to the floor and Jubal seized the opportunity to power himself to his feet.

He came upright as Johnny rushed him from across the circle. The buffalo man came at Jubal like a bull and the smaller man used his momentum and greater weight against him. Snatching an outstretched arm in a two-handed grip, Jubal swung around carrying the big man with him. Johnny was lifted off his feet and hurled against his comrade. Both men went down in a welter of tumbling chairs and shouted curses, Johnny screaming as a flailing arm landed across his broken nose.

'Hell, Tod,' he bellowed, 'you're fightin' him not me damn you.'

Tod pushed his companion away and began to climb to his feet. He was on his knees when Jubal's boot smashed against the point of his jaw. His open mouth was rammed shut, his teeth splintering as they clashed together. He spat blood from cut lips and hurled a chair at Jubal. The smaller man dodged the missile and stepped in close. He swung his arm in a flat curve, fingers held straight and stiff so that the edge of his hand landed across Tod's throat. The big man gagged as his Adam's apple was driven back into his windpipe and a strangled moan burst from his bloody lips. His eyes bugged in his head as he fought for air that could not reach his straining lungs. His hands clawed at his throat as though he sought to tear an air passage into his neck and his face grew purple as he suffocated. An awful gargle belched from his lips as he toppled sideways to lie still on the planks.

Johnny was temporarily shocked into silence by the sheer horror of the moment, but then he shook his head and rushed Jubal again. This time he was more wary and before Jubal could grab him, he drove a punch against the side of the smaller man's head. Jubal was rolling with the blow as it landed, but even so it was powerful enough to jolt him off balance.

He blocked a second punch that threatened to shatter his jaw and danced backwards, trying to lure the buffalo hunter into another crazy charge. Instead, Johnny kicked out, sweeping his foot in a curve that knocked Jubal's legs out from under him. He landed heavily on one shoulder and rolled on to his back as Johnny hurled himself forwards. Jubal raised both legs as the bigger man came down like a human avalanche. His boots landed in Johnny's stomach and he swung his legs up and over his head. Launched by his own momentum, the buffalo hunter flew over Jubal's body to land heavily on the floor beyond. He skidded over the planks, screaming as the rough wood tore a long strip from his lower lip.

He was still face down when Jubal powered himself across the floor. He landed to one side of the groggy buffalo hunter and brought both hands up above his head, linking his fingers so that they formed one powerful fist. He swung down, smashing a bone-jarring blow on to the nape of Johnny's neck. The force of it drove the man's face hard against the floor and Jubal heard the brittle crack of breaking bone. Johnny grunted once like a hurt animal and lay still.

Jubal rolled aside and leapt to his feet, ready to continue the fight. But it was ended: Johnny was knocked cold.

'Mister,' a voice to one side of Jubal exclaimed, 'that was the best fight I ever seen. Now you're under arrest.'

Jubal turned to see a middle-aged man with a straggling

moustache and a silver star pinned to the collar of his black topcoat. He held a Colt, cocked and pointed at Jubal's belly.

'Let's go,' he said, 'an' don't give me any trouble. One wrong move an' you're dead.'

CHAPTER SEVEN

Jubal was allowed to collect his coat and watch before he was escorted at gunpoint from the saloon. The marshal, whose name was apparently Riley, left orders for the two dead buffalo hunters to be carried over to the official mortician, their plain pinewood coffins to be paid for by a collection taken among the onlookers. Jubal himself was required to contribute fifty cents in the interests of civic economy.

'A man gets himself killed around Denver,' Riley explained, 'it's usually in a fight. An' since there's usually a good crowd gathers to watch the fight there don't seem no reason why the spectators shouldn't pay for their fun. Saves the town money, anyway.'

'I guess you'd call it coffin' up,' said Jubal.

It was close to midnight as Riley marched Jubal down mainstreet to the marshal's office. He refused to explain the reasons for the arrest until they were inside the brick building and Jubal, the marshal's Colt pressed into the small of his back, had entered a cell. The door was swung closed and the key turned before Riley agreed to speak.

'Got a message from a friend of mine out East,' he explained, 'said I should look out for someone might be passin' through.' He paused to chew on the ends of his straggling moustache as he watched his prisoner. 'Seems there's a big landowner put out a chaser on the man. Two an' a half thousand dollars he's offerin' for proof the man he wants is dead.'

'That legal money,' Jubal asked carefully, wondering how far he could go in questioning the marshal, 'or just bounty money?'

'That much green stuff makes the dividin' line awful thin,' Riley answered. 'A man could go a long way on two and a half thousand. A whole lot farther than a marshal's pay would take him.'

'Depends on the man,' Jubal said. 'Could be some folks would have trouble sleeping nights if they turned bounty hunter.'

'Friend,' Riley grinned, spitting hairs free of his teeth, 'I've been a county sheriff and a town marshal for thirty years now. You know what I got to show for that time?'

Jubal shook his head.

'I got a good horse I'm gettin' too old to ride,' Riley continued as his eyes adopted a faraway look that suggested he was thinking of times long gone, 'I got a saddle, a Winchester rifle an' a Colt. I got sixty dollars in the bank an' the prospect of gettin' shot one night by some drunken bum who won't even know my name. That's what I got to show for the last thirty years.'

'You sleep nights?' Jubal asked.

'Friend, I sleep rotten. I keep worryin' about tomorrow an' that drunk with the gun.'

'And you think the bounty money will settle that?' asked Jubal.

Riley grinned. 'It'll settle that,' he said. 'It'll give me the money to break free. Maybe buy a small spread someplace, or just live high in my old age. One way or another, it's solid insurance.'

'So how do you earn it?' Jubal demanded thinking fast in a desperate effort to come up with a valid reason why Riley should not gun him down on the spot.

'First I check that I've got the right man,' the marshal answered, eyeing Jubal in speculative fashion. 'That means gettin' a message to Ben Agnew in St. Louis. He's the man offerin' the reward,' he added.

'How long will that take?' Jubal asked. 'I don't want to spend too long in here.'

Riley ignored the implication of innocence in Jubal's remark. 'A few days, maybe a week. You sure fit the bill, though. Message was to look out for a little guy, handy in a fight.'

'That describes a lot of people,' Jubal retorted.

'Yeah,' Riley agreed, 'but there ain't too many dressed up in a dude suit with a derby to match.'

'So I fit the description,' said Jubal, anger lending an edge to his natural intelligence, 'but I'm not the only man in America wearing clothes like these.'

'You're the only one I got at the moment,' Riley replied, 'so you stay there until I know.'

'What's this man supposed to have done?' Jubal wanted to know.

'According to my information,' said Riley, 'he gunned Agnew's wife. Seems they got into some kinda argument an' this fellow pulled a gun an' shot her down.'*

'You ever think that Agnew could be lying?' asked Jubal.

'Friend,' grinned Riley, beginning a fresh assault on the moist ends of his moustache, 'for two and a half grand he's gotta be tellin' the truth. Now you settle down an' make yourself as comfortable as you can.' He turned away towards the front office, calling back over his shoulder, 'If you're not the one I'll apologize later. If you are ...'

'If I am, what?' Jubal shouted.

Riley turned in the doorway, his amiable casualness vanishing as an icy note crept into his voice.

'Then you're gonna try to escape. An' you're gonna get shot dead in the attempt. Now settle down quiet like.'

The wooden door slammed shut behind him and Jubal heard the outer door open and close as the marshal went back on to the street. Furiously, he checked the cell door and the barred window. The door was locked and Jubal could see that he had no chance of breaking through its steel frame. Similarly, the bars of the small window were set solidly into the brick of the walls and without a hacksaw or dynamite there was no way he could work them loose.

He threw himself down on the wooden frame that served as a bed and tried to think of some way to talk himself out of his predicament. He knew that Riley would receive an affirmative reply to his inquiry and his next move would be to shoot Jubal dead. Agnew would send the money and Riley would disappear from Denver leaving behind him one prisoner 'shot while attempting to escape'.

The only good thing about the situation was that Riley

* See – Jubal Cade: Double Cross

57

seemed to view it impersonally. He proved this by arranging for Larry to bring food over from his wife's lodging house.

'After all,' the would-be writer explained, 'you have paid for it.'

'Thanks,' Jubal replied, 'maybe you'd like to ask your wife to bake a saw into a pie next time.'

'That kind of thing only happens in bad novels,' Larry laughed, 'as I should know.'

Jubal spent the better part of that night watching the procedure of the marshal's office. It seemed that Riley had two deputies with whom he divided the nocturnal rounds. They were seldom in the office, obviously relying on the solidity of the cells to prevent any trouble from within, and they returned from their patrolling only long enough to throw the odd drunk into the cells on either side of Jubal's.

As dawn lit up the cold, grey sky Jubal settled down to sleep. Three drunks were snoring around him, sleeping away the excesses of whiskey and the bruises they had picked up during the night. Riley and one of his deputies bedded down in a separate room towards morning, leaving the third deputy to greet the two day men Jubal learned came on duty with the rising sun. A plan was beginning to form in his mind, but it required the solitude of night and anyway he needed sleep.

Morning brought Captain Simms and an angry demand to know what the hell Jubal thought he was doing. The young officer could see his chance of pulling off the coup of arranging a peace treaty with the Cheyenne disappearing.

'There's a simple answer, Captain,' Jubal grinned, deciding that there was no reason why he should suffer alone. 'Just get me out of here and I'll head for Big Wolf's camp.'

His suggestion was only half joking: he knew the kind of influence an Army officer had around a frontier town. There was just a slim chance that Simms might be able to get him out of his predicament.

'No way,' the captain replied. 'I already spoke to Marshal Riley about it and he's determined to keep you inside.'

A cynical smile spread across Jubal's face. 'Yeah,' he murmured, 'I just bet he is.'

'Dammit, Cade,' barked Simms, his temper fraying as he

saw his chance of fame fading, 'you did shoot one man dead and then killed another with your hands.'

'The first one pulled a gun on me,' remarked Jubal mildly, 'and there were two of them in the fight.'

In spite of his unfortunate position he was getting a certain enjoyment from the young soldier's discomfort. He was, after all, the one who had volunteered to ride alone into what was generally regarded as hostile territory to organize a peace talk that would benefit Simms and the citizens of Denver. He felt that the soldier owed him a little more than the brusque irritation he was showing at the moment.

Simms slapped his thigh with a leather gauntlet. 'I know,' he said, 'I put the point to Riley.'

'And he said?' Jubal prompted.

'He said he'd never seen one man lick three buffalo hunters before. And he had other reasons to hold you.'

'You bet he has,' said Jubal, half to himself. 'Two thousand five hundred of them and every one has Abe Lincoln's face on it.'

Simms looked up. 'You mean you're wanted?' he asked.

'I mean,' Jubal replied, deciding to take a chance, 'that there's a man in St. Louis who put a bounty on me.'

'I wish I'd known that earlier,' snapped Simms.

'It's hardly the kind of thing you go around telling people,' grinned Jubal, 'and I'm innocent anyway.'

'Of what?' the soldier asked. 'If I'm to help you at all, then you'd better tell me.'

Jubal decided to put his trust in the captain's desire for promotion and his apparent honesty. He took a deep breath and recounted the story of Agnew, the tragic outcome of their struggle and the resulting manhunt. Captain Simms sat in silence until Jubal had finished then emitted a long, low whistle.

'That's some story,' he said thoughtfully, 'and some enemy. Knowing old Les Riley, I'd say you'll have one hell of a problem getting out of here. On your feet, at least.'

'Suppose I could,' countered Jubal, 'would our agreement still stand?'

'I can't help you break out,' Simms said warily, 'but if you did you might just find a couple of horses and your gear in my office.' He paused. 'Of course, I wouldn't know about it, but the sentries get pretty sleepy towards dawn and the man who brought Big Wolf in for peace talks would be pretty useful to the Army. Might even be that General Standish would put in a word for him with the President.'

Jubal grinned, exposing his broken front teeth; his gambit had worked. He needed an ally on the outside, and preferably one with sufficient influence to cover his tracks and slow any pursuit. It looked as though he had found the man in Captain Simms. Choosing his words with care he mentioned that his saddlebags and rifle were at Lizzie's rooming house, adding that the rifle was a ·30 calibre converted Spencer and that Marshal Riley had confiscated his Colt.

With equal care, Simms pointed out that he knew where the peace officer kept confiscated weapons and opined that he would hardly miss one extra Colt.

Jubal was thoughtful as the young captain departed. He had put the first part of his plan into operation, now it remained to organize the second part before Riley got his answer from St. Louis.

The cellblock was empty as he began to rummage through his pockets. Larry had brought his breakfast and Riley was out of the office to eat his own. That left one deputy on duty and there was no reason to expect him to come looking at his one remaining prisoner now that the drunks had been discharged, sober. Although the marshal had taken Jubal's Colt, he had not searched his prisoner before locking him in the cell. That left Jubal with two pockets full of ·30 calibre cartridges and he gave silent thanks that he preferred to keep his ammunition in his coat pockets rather than in the more conventional belt loops. Keeping his ears open for any movement outside, he piled the cartridges on the bunk and pulled a handkerchief from his pants pocket. One by one, he bit the metal heads loose from their jackets and emptied the contents of the shell cases on to the handkerchief. When he had finished a pile of black gunpowder and cordite lay on the square of cloth. He gathered the four corners together and tied them in a firm knot before tucking the fist-sized bundle under the bunk. Then he replaced the shell cases and bullet heads in his pockets and settled down to wait for nightfall.

The day was uneventful. Riley had not yet got an answer to his inquiry and it was obvious that Captain Simms's interest in Jubal was making the ageing marshal think twice about gunning him down out of hand.

In the evening Larry brought him more food and the half-puzzled, half-knowing comment that a man had turned up at the rooming house to collect Jubal's gear.

'Funny thing,' remarked the man from Connecticut as he waited for Jubal to finish his meal, 'but I'd have sworn he was a soldier. Wasn't in uniform, but he acted like one.'

'He was most likely a deputy,' suggested Jubal, thankful that Simms seemed to be playing his part in their deal and nervous that Larry might give it away.

'I never seen him before,' replied Larry, 'but I guess it's none of my business.'

'Who else would collect the stuff?' Jubal inquired blandly.

'I don't know,' the other answered, 'an' I guess I don't care either if you're not worried.'

'I don't plan to lose any sleep over it,' Jubal said easily. 'Right now I've got other things on my mind.'

'Yeah,' Larry murmured as he gathered up the empty plates, 'I suppose you have.'

He left Jubal alone to sip the coffee delivered with the meal. It had been poured into a tin mug that served for both water and coffee and was left in the cell when knives, forks and any other potentially dangerous implements were removed. Jubal was grateful: the mug was important to his escape plan.

He waited until Riley and the deputies had left on their nightly rounds and after making sure the place was deserted began to hammer the mug against the window ledge. It was thin metal and a dent quickly appeared in the rim; soon it was indented in a vee shape that suited Jubal's purpose. He pulled his shirt loose and ripped a two foot long strip from the tails before tucking the ragged ends back into his pants. Then, taking the bundle of explosive powder from beneath

61

the bunk, he arranged the various items in a line on the blanket.

It was full night outside with all the concomitant sounds of a boisterous, violent city as Jubal began to assemble the package. He hoped that some outburst of trouble would keep the marshal and his deputies occupied while he worked and listened carefully for any sound from the front office that might indicate their return.

He loosened the knotted ends of the handkerchief slightly and then pushed the bundle into the coffee mug, tamping it carefully down until it was jammed hard against the restraining sides of the mug. The strip of torn shirt served to lash the powder-filled mug to the cell door, where it was firmly held against the lock. The indented section of the rim was uppermost and Jubal paused to survey his handiwork before lighting a cheroot. He puffed the thin, black cylinder of tobacco into fiery life before breaking it off about an inch from the tip. Several inhalations of the pungent smoke ensured a fiercely glowing tip before he pushed it gingerly down through the indentation of the mug's rim into the bundle of powder. Jumping back across the cell, he snatched up the blanket and draped it over the lethal handmade bomb. Then he crouched in the farthest corner to await the results of his handiwork.

They were not long in coming. A violent explosion sent a sheet of bright flame leaping out from the cell door as acrid smoke billowed across the room. The blanket lifted back, spraying sparks and the bitter smell of burning wool around Jubal's head.

The lock shattered outwards as the mug shot back like a cannon ball, bouncing off the wall and rattling noisily around the bars. Before it came to rest Jubal had powered himself to his feet, his shoulder slamming hard against the cell door. The metal frame gave under the impact and he flew out, careening against the far wall. He darted back to collect his topcoat and then hurled himself through the outer door. The blanket had muffled a certain amount of the detonation, but Jubal could hear noises outside that could mean an alert marshal ready to earn his bounty money the easy way. He paused long enough to snatch his shoulder holster from a peg on the wall and then opened the door on to the street.

He came face to face with a running deputy, a Colt clutched in his right hand.

'Sorry, friend,' Jubal grated as he seized the man's wrist, pulling him forwards into the jailhouse. His knee came up in a short, brutal movement that elicited a gasp of raw pain from the peace officer as he doubled over, clutching at his agonized groin. Jubal brought his free hand down, the fist balled, on to the back of the man's neck. At the same time his knee was lifting again, so that the deputy's skull was pounded between the two opposed forces. The man grunted once and slumped on to the floor of the office. Jubal snatched the pistol from his hand and leapt through the doorway.

A small crowd was gathering, attracted by the random chance of excitement that promised to interrupt another slow night of drinking and whoring.

'Jailbreak!' Jubal shouted, hoping that no one in the crowd would recognize him. 'They got the deputy. Where's Riley?'

'Riley?' the nearest onlooker gaped. 'Last I saw him was in the Silver Dollar.'

'Somebody go fetch him,' Jubal shouted, calculating that any firm command could establish dominance over the confused men milling around the jail. 'Hurry!'

The urgency in his voice sent several watchers running in different directions as the others flooded forwards across the boardwalk. Jubal took the opportunity to move through them up the street, away from the smoking cell and the groaning deputy marshal. He walked without seeming to hurry, but still managed to make good time as he paced the walkway towards the Army bivouac. As he went, men jostled him in their rush to find out what new excitement was promised. And as they passed him he added to their anticipation with promises of the biggest jailbreak Denver had ever witnessed. As much as was possible, he clung to shadows between the well-lit saloons and was grateful that the confusion of his escape and the usual turmoil of a frontier town allowed him to move unnoticed in the direction of the camp.

Before long he was off mainstreet and moving through the

darker back roads. The mud he had encountered on his earlier visit was frozen now and the icy wind reminded him that Colorado was still deep in the grip of winter. Crossing the river and riding northwest to the Cheyenne camp would not be easy. But, he mused, infinitely preferable to sitting out the time in jail until confirmation of Agnew's reward came in and Marshal Riley decided to claim it.

He thrust his hands, his right still clutching the deputy's Colt, deep into the pockets of his topcoat and concentrated on traversing the ridges and potholes of the frozen road.

The Army camp was well-lit as he approached and Jubal decided to make an unobtrusive entrance. He moved around the outer ring of tents, staying in the shadows as he watched the patrolling guards. Picking his time so that two sentries were at the farther ends of their patrol areas, he began to inch his way across the frozen ground using the darkness and the overhanging tent flaps as cover. Once he was inside the perimeter he rose to his feet and walked casually through the serried ranks of frost-crystalled canvas towards the headquarters building. The sound of voices murmured through the bivouac, the low hum punctuated by the snorting of horses as they moved, restless in the chill night air, around their corral. An occasional soldier moved past Jubal, huddled in an Army greatcoat and more interested in reaching his destination than in the silent figure moving through the camp.

He reached the captain's quarters and, without knocking, slipped inside. Simms looked up as Jubal entered. He had been studying a map of the area and a mug of steaming coffee stood by his elbow. He gestured at the pot.

'Coffee? You look pretty cold.'

'Thanks,' Jubal grinned, helping himself to a mug, 'I am. Things are pretty hot in town, though.'

Simms looked worried. 'I hope no one's hurt.'

Jubal shook his head as he sat down.

'One deputy's feeling pretty sore and Riley's going to need a new lock on his cell, but that's all. No permanent damage done.'

'Anyone see you coming in?' Simms asked.

'No. The place was too busy to notice when I left. And I

didn't think you'd want me going up to the sentries to say I was here.'

Simms looked pleased.

'Good. The fewer people know where you're headed, the better.' He paused to sip his coffee. 'I got your gear from the rooming house and stowed it in my quarters.' He pointed to the door set into the rear wall of the office as he spoke. 'Your rifle and the handgun are both there and I've put a couple of boxes of shells in your saddlebag.'

'What about food and horses?' Jubal asked.

'We can cut two mounts out of the corral,' Simms replied, 'and I've dumped enough provisions with your gear to see you through.'

'Thanks,' Jubal grinned. 'Let's hope they serve their purpose.'

'Let's hope you serve mine,' said Simms. 'I took a hell of a long chance helping you. The kind that could get me drummed out of the Army. Just don't let me down.'

'I'll do my best,' the smaller man replied. 'After all, I've got a vested interest: it'll be me who gets strung up if I let you down.'

'I guess that's right,' the officer remarked, a grim smile playing over his face. 'Let's hope it works out well for both of us.'

'Yeah,' Jubal said, moving towards the captain's sleeping quarters and the gear stashed there. 'There's something I'd like you to do after I've gone.'

He pulled the two gold-filled saddlebags from among the other items and handed them to Simms.

'I'd like you to put this into a bank, then arrange to have it transferred to the Lenz Clinic in St. Louis. I'll write a note to go with it.'

As he scribbled a brief message to Dr. Lenz he explained the situation to Simms. The young captain agreed to handle the arrangements for the transfer and Jubal hoped that he was as trustworthy as he seemed. There was little choice, however, as the heavy saddlebags would slow him down and if he should die out in the snow country the gold would prove useless to everyone. He preferred to take a chance on Simms and trust that the money would be sent to the clinic.

'Thanks, Captain,' he smiled as he handed over the note, 'I'm grateful to you.'

Simms returned the smile and stowed the saddlebags in a small safe. He turned, his right hand extended.

'Good luck, Cade,' he said as they shook hands. 'Now let's go.'

Jubal collected his gear and the two men walked out of the office towards the corral. Simms dismissed the trooper on guard, explaining that he wanted to show his civilian friend the horse herd with a view to Jubal acting as a supplier of Army mounts. When the soldier had disappeared into the darkness they saddled one of the heavy animals and loaded the other with provisions. Simms lifted a corral pole free of its post so that it would look as though the horses had been stolen and stood silently watching as Jubal led the two animals clear of the camp.

He walked them away from Denver until the bivouac had faded into the night, only the dull glow of its fires showing through the darkness. Then he mounted and began the lonely ride in search of the Cheyenne camp. He was by no means certain that he could find it again and less sure of how long it would take. Still, he told himself, the chance was better than the certainty of a bullet back in the town jail. He huddled down into his topcoat and rode on through the snow.

A little over two hours after Jubal had left the bivouac Marshal Riley rode in at the head of a posse. He had seven buffalo hunters at his back and could see his chance of making two and a half thousand dollars disappearing into the night. He stormed into the captain's office demanding to know if Simms had had anything to do with the jailbreak.

Captain Simms denied it.

'So tell me,' Riley snarled, 'why the hell you were so interested in him?'

'He claimed to have influence with the Cheyenne,' Simms replied calmly, 'so I asked him to scout for me. Before you threw him in jail,' he added.

'Damn' injun lover,' grunted Riley. 'Could be he's headed that way right now.'

'I wouldn't know,' said the officer, 'and I'd like to get some sleep.'

'I'd like to know who the hell collected his gear,' Riley muttered, eyeing the captain suspiciously, 'an' who's gonna help him get out of town. If he ain't gone already.'

Simms shrugged, maintaining his stance of non-involvement.

'Sorry, marshal, but I can't help you.'

'Don't worry,' grated Riley, turning to leave the office, 'I'll find him.'

CHAPTER EIGHT

Les Riley spent the night combing Denver from top to bottom. At the head of a growing band of angry men he took apart anywhere that seemed a likely hiding place. The marshal was furious at the thought of losing his bounty money and his pride was hurt by Jubal's unforeseen escape. Although he suspected Captain Simms of helping his prisoner, the peace officer was in no position to voice his feelings to his followers; nor did he wish to reveal that the hunted man was worth two and a half thousand in greenbacks.

So instead he devoted himself to stoking the buffalo hunters' natural suspicion of anyone remotely sympathetic to the Indians. By the time dawn broke over the town, Riley had a posse of twenty men lusting after Jubal's blood. The fugitive was blamed for most of the crimes committed in Denver over the past few weeks, branded a renegade supporter of the Indians and held responsible for any recent outrages against white men. The only valid accusation levelled at Jubal during the night-long hate campaign was the killing of the three hunters that had led to his present plight. And that had been in self-defence. Riley, however, used his position as town marshal and the buffalo men's love of a fight to incense them against the stranger. As the sun rose above the snow-covered plain Riley swung into the saddle of a big bay stallion and led a band of armed men out of Denver in pursuit of his quarry.

Before leaving, the marshal had sent messages out along the telegraph wires linking Denver with the surrounding townships. His fellow peace officers were warned of a dangerous killer on the loose and given Jubal's description. Riley galloped out knowing that Jubal would be arrested if he strayed into any of the settlements within easy distance of Denver.

The last message, however, was the one that Marshal

Riley had awaited most eagerly. The slip of paper carrying the words hurriedly scribbled by the telegraph operator was folded carefully into an inside pocket of the marshal's coat and he had not mentioned it to anyone.

The note said simply: DESCRIPTION FITS. DELIVER CADE OR CERTIFICATE OF DEATH. REWARD YOURS. It was signed AGNEW.

Beneath the woollen muffler that obscured the lower half of his face, Riley's lips were set in a determined line that was partly a smile of anticipation and partly a grimace. While his riders had saddled their mounts he had detailed several experienced trackers to circle the town, quartering the ground for signs of Jubal's escape route. Although the early morning snowfall had done a lot to obscure his tracks, the pursuers were skilled enough to guess that he would most likely head north and that, allied to their belief that he was a renegade Indian-lover, was sufficient to persuade them that he would attempt to cross the Platte in an effort to find shelter with his Cheyenne friends.

Several miles out of town the trackers found the remains of a fire on the east bank of the river. There were signs of two horses and a double line of hoof prints pointing north. Without stopping, Riley led the posse on through the deep snow.

Jubal, meanwhile, was making the best time he could through the drifts. It was a clear day with no sign of impending snow and the crusted surface of the all-embracing whiteness around him made for easier going than the ride into Denver. He was all too aware that it also made for easier tracking. There was no way, though, that he could hide the twin lines of broken snow stretching out behind him so he concentrated on moving ahead as swiftly as possible. Every so often he turned to scan the terrain at his back. It was difficult to distinguish any dividing line between the iron grey sky and the dazzling snowfields, but the blinding clarity of the winter-bound plains country at least ensured that he would see any pursuers.

Captain Simms had included a charcoal stick in the provisions he had set out and Jubal had used it to blacken his cheekbones and upper eye lids. Although he had never experienced it himself, he was aware of the danger of snow blindness and was wary of succumbing to the monotony of the flat, white country that could easily lead him into wandering in sightless circles until Riley and his men caught up.

Utilizing his memory of the large-scale map in the Army office and the smaller one Simms had given him, he was planning to head north along the bank of the Platte until he reached a crossing point the army officer had pointed out. There, he would strike west, moving into the mountains and hoping that he could either find Big Wolf's village or be found by the Cheyenne. Little Bear had promised to maintain a watch for Jubal's return and the young doctor was pretty certain that the Cheyenne would find him before he located their village. But either way he still had the problem of the posse to contend with. He had no wish to lead his pursuers to the Indian camp, nor to wander himself until they caught up.

He moved on, hoping that he could head off into the shelter of the mountains before Riley and the buffalo hunters came in sight.

He saw them the second day out of Denver. Darkness and the bone-numbing cold had forced him to shelter in the lee of a cluster of boulders jutting from the river bank. He had lit a small fire after feeding the two horses and draping them in heavy Army blankets. Then he had wrapped himself in a blanket and settled down to eat. He awoke at dawn and quickly saddled the animals as he chewed on a strip of dried beef. He was pushing on through the snow when a rearward glance showed a group of figures, dark against the whiteness, moving behind him. Jubal estimated that they were about three miles back and cursed the first stop he had made to eat and check his supplies. It had seemed necessary at the time, but now he realized that the posse was riding unencumbered by packhorses and must have pushed ahead at the fastest pace possible.

Now that the group was within sighting distance, he realized, he must have been spotted. And if he could not keep up his lead the long-range buffalo guns would bring him down like so much carrion for Riley to pick over.

He made a fast decision and cut the packhorse loose. If it could not make its own way back to Denver then the posse would most likely pick it up. Living off the few supplies he carried in his own saddlebags would be difficult, but preferable to risking a bullet in the back at the expense of allowing the horse to slow him down. Set free, the animal chose to follow its companion and fell into line behind. Jubal ignored it as he kicked his own mount into the floundering walk that was the best pace it could manage through the snow.

There was a dream-like quality to the chase as fugitive and pursuers moved in slow motion across the empty, white landscape. Speed was impossible and the usual perspectives of the terrain were obliterated by the blanketing snow. Jubal's path was the more difficult as he was breaking fresh ground while the posse could follow his track, riding across snow that was flattened by his horses' hooves. He was forced to glance frequently at the map Simms had given him for fear of missing the ford in his haste while the posse had simply to keep on coming using his figure as the target.

They continued in this fashion for two more hours before the first shot rang out.

Jubal heard the dull cough of a ·50 calibre Sharps and risked turning to check the distance. The buffalo hunters had closed the gap and one had reined in his horse to try a long distance shot. Jubal had heard that the big guns could power a slug for a mile and even though it was difficult to judge distance, he calculated that the marksman was too far back to hit him. Even so, he saw a plume of snow rise up to the right of his trail several hundred yards behind and urged his panting mount to greater effort. The ford was about half a mile ahead: he hoped he could reach it in time.

A mile behind him Riley was lashing his horse in pursuit.

'Damn it, Tod,' he yelled over his shoulder, 'don't waste shells unless you know you can hit him.'

'Figgered it was worth a try,' the buffalo hunter shouted back as he pushed a fresh cartridge into the breech of the Sharps.

'Leave the figgerin' to me,' snarled Riley, 'you just shoot

when I tell you.'

Tad spat on to the snow and pushed his horse on after the others, sliding his rifle back into its protective rawhide sheath.

Up ahead, a flurry of falling snow hid Jubal from sight. The drifting flakes grew stronger and the posse was forced to steer on Jubal's tracks.

'I reckon he's headin' for Fisher's Crossing, Les,' shouted a rider, 'that's about the only place he can break off this side of Cheyenne.'

'You could be right,' Riley called back. 'If we lose the trail we'll head for there an' catch him before he joins up with his injun friends.'

'If this snow keeps up,' the other man replied, 'we'll have to stop there.'

'I ain't stoppin' until Cade's the wrong side of a bullet,' Riley barked.

'Hell, Les,' came the voice from behind the marshal, 'any-one'd think there was money in this.'

Riley stayed silent, but his right hand slipped instinctively inside his coat where his fingers closed around the note from Agnew. Beneath his muffler his lips parted in a wolfish smile.

'Friend,' he muttered to himself, 'you just don't know how right you are.'

CHAPTER NINE

The posse was hidden by the falling snow when Jubal came abreast of the ford. He recognized the spot from the map and the description Simms had given him and hauled his pony around towards the river. He walked the animal down the shallow slope of the river bank and then kicked it forwards into the water. The Platte was no more than a foot deep at this point and although the water was freezing very little ice had formed on the surface. The pack animal followed, splashing over in Jubal's wake. Some distance in front he could see the faint outlines of tumbled rock through the falling snow and decided to keep moving until he could find suitable cover. It was possible that he could lose Riley and his men in the foothills and the snow, but if not he wanted a place to make a stand. His horse could not go on much farther and he had no wish to find himself afoot in the snow-covered mountains.

His eyes were forced into tight slits as he peered out through the enveloping flakes. The vague outline of some kind of trail showed through the snow and he chose to follow it, heading towards the rocks. The one good thing about the poor visibility, he thought, was that the buffalo hunters would lose the advantage of their longer-ranged guns. In this kind of weather Jubal's own Spencer would be as effective as the big Sharps.

He rode on, looking for cover.

Behind him, Riley was approaching the crossing. The marshal reined in at the river bank, his eyes, red-rimmed from lack of sleep, scanned the tracks leading down to the water and out the other side. He raised an arm above his head and signalled the posse to follow him across. In single file, the twenty-one men splashed through the waters of the Platte, their hunters' eyes probing the far bank for their quarry.

'Hell, Dave,' grunted one rider to the man who had come up alongside him, 'ole Les sure wants this one bad.'

'I never known him to follow another so far, Andy,' came the reply.

'It's like his pension depended on it,' Andy said. 'You'd think the little guy had robbed a bank or something.'

They fell silent as they followed Riley into the jumble of rocks beyond the opposite bank. Night was not far off and they knew they would soon be forced to stop. The darkness and the cold would render hunters and hunted alike immobile until morning when they could take up the trail again. It was not long before Riley reluctantly called a halt. Even the embittered marshal was forced to recognize the impossibility of chasing Jubal in the dark, so he chose to make camp and rest the horses in readiness for an early start the next day.

Jubal kept moving until the last of the daylight faded. He found a cluster of sheltering boulders that provided both a windbreak and a screen that would hide his campfire from view. He led his horse into the stone circle and then brought the pack animal in. He scouted on foot for wood and succeeded in gathering a double armful of branches from the trees flanking the trail. He lit a fire and set several strips of beef to char over the flames before rubbing down both horses and covering them with the warming Army blankets. He fed them a little grain from his saddlebags and spread a groundsheet near the fire. Then he settled down to eat himself. Afterwards he lit a cheroot and leaned back against the rocks to contemplate his next move.

He knew the posse could not be far behind and the buffalo hunters would know the country better than he did. That meant he had to rely on staying ahead of them or facing them in a fight. Although he was perfectly prepared to shoot it out, he preferred to avoid a pitched battle for the obvious reason that he was badly outnumbered.

By the light of his campfire he studied the map, noting that his estimate of Big Wolf's position necessitated a swing to the southwest. That would take him close to a small lake that fed into the Green River. He stared at the blue circle indicating the lake as a plan began to form in his mind.

74

At the same time, Riley was staring at the message from Agnew and planning how to spend the reward money.

Jubal's animal-like reflexes woke him as dawn broke. He was covered with a dusting of snow and the stubble on his cheeks was frosted with ice crystals as he threw his blanket off and rose to his feet. His breath came in steaming gusts in the clear, cold morning air and he noted that it looked like another snow-free day. That would make his going easier, but also mean his trail would be clear behind him. He shrugged in resignation as he fed the horses and watered them with snow melted over his rekindled fire. He decided to forego coffee in favour of haste and as soon as the two horses had finished eating he saddled the fresher pack animal.

The pony he had been riding was exhausted and chose to remain within the rocky circle as Jubal prepared to leave. He dropped a half-full sack of grain on to the snow and rode out hoping the animal would survive. Then he headed towards the lake.

Riley, meanwhile, was kicking protesting buffalo hunters awake in preparation for another day's chase.

'Dammit, Les,' complained the man called Andy, 'ain't we followed him far enough?'

'No, we ain't,' snarled Riley, warming his hands around a mug of coffee, 'we'll follow him until hell freezes over.'

'Les,' remarked the hunter called Dave, 'I got news for you. It's froze over already.'

'Yeah,' agreed Andy, 'an' we'll freeze with it if we go on.'

'All right, quitters,' Riley's mouth was twisted in an ugly line beneath his frosted moustache, 'so you go home. An' tell yore pals you let an injun-lovin' renegade go free.'

'Aw shit, Les,' said Andy, 'we keep on after him an' we'll be shakin' hands with his injun friends.'

'An' they'll be shakin' our scalps,' muttered Dave.

'Ah, keep yore hair on,' Riley grunted, 'if you want to quit, then go now. Don't keep talkin' about it.'

'OK, Les,' it was Andy, shamefaced, 'I guess I've had enough. I'm quittin' right now.'

He rose to his feet, hefting his saddle as he stared at Riley. 'You ain't never chased anyone so hard before, Les. We're into injun land right now an' we don't have enough food to keep goin' much farther.'

Dave rose, too. He joined his friend. 'He's right, Les. It ain't humanly possible to keep on one more day. I say we quit now.'

Riley spat into the fire. 'I say you're both stinkin' cowards. We came after Cade because he killed two of yore people an' because he's a lousy injun-lover. I intend to get him an' it don't matter how far I have to chase him: I'm gonna bring him back.'

The two buffalo hunters eyed Riley nervously, angered by his insults but unsure of their ground when it came to facing down a town marshal in front of witnesses.

'Oh hell,' muttered Andy, 'you go yore own way, Les. Me, I'm headin' back to Denver.'

'Me too,' Dave agreed. 'One pint-sized jail-breaker ain't worth all this trouble.'

They moved over to the tethered horses, avoiding the curious looks of the other men. Riley watched them saddle up and mount, then stood staring after them as they rode back down the trail to Fisher's Crossing. When they were out of sight he saddled his own horse.

'I got a message for them to take back,' he called over his shoulder as he spurred after them.

Andy and Dave were riding easily and Riley overtook them as they reached the river. The two men reined in as he came alongside.

'What is it, Les?' queried Andy.

'Got a message for you take back,' grunted Riley.

His hand came out of the pocket of his heavy cloth coat holding a cocked pistol.

'I don't like quitters.'

He squeezed the trigger as he stuck the muzzle against Andy's ribs. The buffalo hunter was hurled sideways off his horse, a look of disbelieving surprise on his face. Riley swung his own pony around as Dave clawed desperately at the rawhide wrap that protected his rifle.

'Les,' he shouted, 'what the hell are you doin'?'

76

'Killing quitters,' snarled the marshal, 'an' protectin' my investment.'

He thumbed the hammer a second time and grinned as Dave doubled over his saddle horn. The buffalo hunter was badly wounded but still alive and he clung to his pony in a frantic attempt to escape. Riley pushed his own mount up to side Dave's and pressed the gun barrel against the man's head. He fired as the two animals splashed into the river, then hauled his own horse to a stop as the other galloped through the water. Dave was blown from the saddle, his shattered skull tinging the drift ice to crimson as his body floated south.

Riley kicked his horse up the bank, pausing to check that Andy was dead. The man was sprawled in the snow, red blood frothing from the wound in his side as sightless eyes stared at the empty sky.

'Tough,' grunted the marshal, 'but I told you I didn't like quitters. An' I do want Cade.'

He rode back to the camp, explaining that he had asked the two men to relay a message to his deputies in Denver saying that he would be gone for several days more. The posse grumbled some at the prospect of staying out in the open but no one dared face down Riley's furious glare. Instead, they mounted and rode out on Jubal's trail.

Jubal had used the time afforded by Riley's murderous foray to press ahead in the direction of the lake and by mid-morning he could see the shimmer of ice through the trees. The hours since dawn had taken him higher into the Rockies where the broken ground made the going a little easier than across the flat snowfields of the plains. By now the sun was shining between the fir trees, throwing brilliant flashes of light up off the snow. Jubal reached the lake about noon and dismounted on the bank, eyeing the expanse of sparkling ice stretching out before him. The water was about a quarter mile across and its covering ice looked thick enough to support a rider. He decided against taking the chance and instead led his pony down to the edge. Gingerly, he stepped on to the frozen surface and began to walk around the perimeter of the lake. He was not sure how much time he had before the posse caught up, but hoped that he could get at least half

77

way around before he was spotted.

Luck was with him and he succeeded in traversing the lake before any riders came into view. The ice was too hard to record his passing so all that Riley and his men saw was the line of hoofmarks leading to the ice's edge and, on the far side, a line leading out.

Jubal, meanwhile, had tethered his horse up the bank under the sheltering trees and was crouched behind a tall pine whose branches hung down into the snow, hiding him from view.

He watched silently as Riley broke through the trees, arrow-straight on Jubal's trail. The marshal reined in at the lake's edge and eyed the opposite bank. He spotted the tracks leading up through the snow and yelled at the riders behind him.

'There! He crossed the lake and headed through the trees. The sonofabitch can't be much farther ahead.'·

He kicked his horse out on to the ice, shouting for the others to follow him. The buffalo hunters came on more reluctantly, walking their mounts cautiously on to the frozen surface. Their courage grew as they progressed farther across and found the ice firm. Riley was several yards ahead, driving his animal in a sliding, slipping canter over the lake. Shouting jubilantly, the others followed him.

Jubal rested the barrel of the Spencer carefully on a low-hanging branch and sighted. He eased back the hammer and took up the trigger slack. A fraction more pressure was applied to the delicate mechanism and the rifle barked, the echo of its discharge ringing from the pines surrounding the lake. Riley's horse bucked wildly as the first bullet ploughed into the ice at its feet. The marshal was still fighting to control the animal as Jubal levered a second shell into the breech and fired again. He hit his target: the spot where the first bullet had struck. Three more shots smashed into the ice in fast succession and a long, ragged crack appeared.

Riley had his horse under control as the buffalo hunters grouped around him. Several jumped from their saddles, seeking firmer footing in order to answer Jubal's fire. As they unlimbered their own rifles Jubal emptied his gun into the ice.

He reloaded fast and swung the barrel in a short arc, working the lever action and triggering the Spencer with near-mechanical rapidity.

His bullets thudded into the frozen lake, ignoring the posse. But all around the confused hunters a network of cracks was appearing. Riley saw the danger first and pushed his horse into a desperate gallop for the bank. Behind him the buffalo men realized what was happening and sought safety on their own animals. Jubal paid no attention to the bullets that spattered the trees around his vantage point, concentrating instead on shattering the ice with his own shots.

The milling horses stamping the surface in the centre of the lake aided his purpose and suddenly a yawning gap showed in the ice.

Two men screamed as their footing slid from under them, tipping them into the freezing water. They disappeared beneath the shifting ice as three horses crashed through, carrying their riders with them. Jubal put down a pattern of shots that forced Riley to swing off to one side and then paused to reload the Spencer as he watched the confusion in front of him.

His fire had completely wrecked the delicate balance between water and ice so that the entire surface of the lake was breaking up. Buffalo men pitched shouting into the water, their clutching fingers sliding off slippery ice-floes as they were dragged down. A few clung to tossing chunks of ice until the cold and the movement numbed their grip and threw them free. Horses squealed in panic, kicking out so that the moving surface shifted still further until they, too, slithered into the water.

About four men, led by Riley, made the safety of the far bank. The others went under the ice as it broke up or clung helplessly to floating chunks as lake water lapped around their bodies, freezing them where they lay. One man screamed as he sought to fire his rifle with one hand.

'Stinkin' injun-lover!'

Jubal grinned coldly as he sighted on the fragile ice.

'I don't stink like a buffalo hunter,' he muttered, 'so take a bath.'

He squeezed the trigger and watched the man's temporary

refuge disintegrate, dropping him into the water. He sank from view, dragged down by the weight of his winter clothing.

Jubal ran back to his horse and mounted. Before Riley and the other survivors could group themselves he wanted to get away from the icy battlefield.

CHAPTER TEN

Two miles away from the lake, Jubal allowed his horse to slow down to its own pace. He had ridden the animal hard in his dash from the frozen battleground and was wary of winding the big grey in case he should need a sudden burst of speed. He was fairly sure that Riley and the other survivors would lick their wounds before coming after him, but wanted to put as much distance as possible between them. Although he knew he would feel no compunction, no pang of conscience should he be forced to kill the lawman, he was loath to do so. Gunning down a buffalo hunter in a fair fight was all right, but he did not know what repercussions the slaying of a legally appointed marshal might have and he had no wish to add another notch to his tally of enemies. So he pushed on through the snowbound trees hoping that he could stay ahead of Riley.

He was picking his way carefully through a deep-drifted pine break when figures materialized around him. They were draped in heavy buffalo skin cloaks, with frost-whitened feathers standing up out of their braided hair: Indians. Jubal recognized Little Bear, riding slightly ahead of his companions, a broad smile showing on his dark face.

'Jubal,' he shouted, his right hand raised palm outwards, 'you came back.'

'Me and a few others,' Jubal replied, casting a glance back over his shoulder, 'let's get the hell out of here.'

'The buffalo men?' Little Bear queried. 'We heard fighting. I sent men to scout the lake. They came back saying the whites went under the ice.' He laughed. 'The ice you broke, Jubal.'

'Yeah. But there were some got out.'

His words were punctuated by the booming explosion of a heavy calibre rifle and a shower of dislodged snow fell from

81

the branches above his head as the hurriedly aimed bullet whined off through the trees.

The Cheyenne evaporated into the snowy landscape like so many shadows. Little Bear reached out to grab Jubal's reins and hauled horse and man off the trail into the shelter of the trees from which vantage point Jubal could see Riley and three of the surviving posse fanning out across the trail. A bow string twanged and an arrow sprouted suddenly from the shoulder of the gunman. He yelled, dropping his rifle into the snow as he clutched at the shaft protruding from his body.

'No!' Jubal shouted, 'don't kill them.'

The Cheyenne warriors were spread out under the pines, their bows notched with arrows ready to pour into the white men. But Jubal's shout prompted them to hold their fire, their dark eyes moving between the targets and the small figure on the grey horse. Little Bear bellowed a gutteral command and no more arrows were unleashed. He eyed Jubal quizzically, clearly unsure why his friend should wish to save the lives of his enemies.

'If you kill them,' Jubal said urgently, 'there will be more come looking for them. When the bodies are found they will come looking for your village. Let them go and tell their people the Cheyenne spared their lives.'

'Better to kill them now,' replied Little Bear, 'and fight their friends later.'

The wounded buffalo hunter was hanging on to his horse in the open space between a ring of trees. He was groaning with the pain of the arrow wound and obviously uncertain what would happen if he tried to make a break for cover. His fellows were holding their fire, partly because they were unsure of the Indians' positions, partly because they did not know how many Cheyenne they faced.

Jubal turned to Little Bear.

'You wanted to talk peace. One of these men is a chief in Denver. If you kill him there will be no peace.'

Little Bear thought for a long moment before replying. 'You are right, Jubal. We let them go.'

He gestured to the other braves, who lowered their bows,

although they kept the weapons in readiness for swift usage.

'Riley,' shouted Jubal, 'if you turn around and head back to Denver you might just stay alive. Stay here and I'll guarantee it'll be for ever.'

'Why the hell should I take yore word?' Riley shouted. 'We come a long way for you, Cade.'

'You don't have too much choice,' replied Jubal. 'You start shooting and you're dead. You don't stand a chance out in the open.'

'I could maybe get you, injun-lover,' Riley answered bitterly.

'Maybe you could, but if you did you'd never live to enjoy that reward.'

Jubal's comment brought a sudden burst of questions from the men accompanying Riley. None of them knew anything about a reward and its revelation – especially in these circumstances – prompted them to question the marshal. The doubts raised by Jubal and the awkward situation set them firmly in favour of a strategic withdrawal from the murderous fire they knew could erupt from among the pine trees.

'All right, Cade,' Riley yelled, 'this time you win. Just remember I'm lookin' for you. An' sometime I'm gonna get you.'

'Just keep it up,' Jubal called, 'and see what happens. Perhaps you'll live to a ripe old age; providing you turn around right now.'

Reluctantly, Riley pulled his horse's head around and moved back down the trail. Little Bear signalled to his warriors and they moved out of the trees to form a defensive barrier between Jubal and the other white men. The three buffalo hunters could see that they would not stand a chance against the Indians and began to ride away.

'Wait,' Jubal shouted.

They reined in as Riley sat his horse in the centre of the trail, naked hatred showing in his eyes. Jubal moved towards the group.

'You won't get far with that arrow in you,' he called. 'Better let me take it out.'

'We don't need no help from a cruddy renegade,' snarled

83

one of the men.

'You may not,' answered Jubal, 'but your friend does. He won't last to daybreak if I don't dress that wound.'

'So what makes you the medical expert?' rasped the first spokesman.

'A few years training as a doctor,' grinned Jubal, untying his black medical valise from behind his saddle and holding it up in the air so the three men could see it clearly. He was not particularly sorry for the wounded man, but felt that a gesture of help might stand him in good stead later on when he returned to Denver.

The hunters were less sure, until a groan from the wounded man made them realize that Jubal could easily be right.

'Come on, Tad,' said the one holding the man upright in his saddle, 'it can't do no harm. An' it don't look like Jesse'll last if that shaft stays where it is.'

Jesse opened his eyes. 'He's right, Tad. Fer God's sake let him take it out.'

Tad spat on the snow, glowering at Jubal.

'All right, squaw man, do yore stuff.'

Jubal heeled his pony forwards so that he came up alongside Riley. As he did so the marshal reached out, as though to grab him. The Cheyenne bows came up, seven of them pointed at Riley's chest.

'I wouldn't try anything, marshal,' said Jubal easily. 'You make the wrong move and things could get prickly.'

'Damn you, Cade,' snarled the frustrated bounty hunter, 'there'll come a day when I catch up with you.'

'Maybe so,' answered Jubal as he dismounted, 'but don't count on it.'

He helped the wounded man to climb down off his horse and organized the spreading of a groundsheet on the snow. The wound was not serious, the man's several layers of winter clothing having slowed the arrow's velocity so that it had penetrated only slightly. But the cold and the shock had taken a drastic toll, resulting in a weakened condition that, combined with loss of blood, might easily kill him. Certainly, Jubal thought, he was unlikely to survive the night with the arrow still in him.

He used Jesse's own knife to cut the wooden shaft close to the man's coat and then, as Tad and the other hunter started a fire, gently removed the clothing to expose the stump of the arrow. The blazing branches gave off enough heat to keep Jesse warm when his grimy shoulder was bared and Jubal prayed that he was not too far into shock to survive the operation. Although it was relatively minor, he had seen too many men succumb to the pain and secondary infections to be sure of saving Jesse's life. None the less, he opened his medical bag and prepared to remove the arrow. The belligerent buffalo hunter offered his companion a wad of tobacco to bite on and as his teeth clamped into the black stick of evil-smelling stuff, Jubal cleansed a scalpel in pure alcohol.

Riley sat silently on his horse, watching the scene as the two buffalo men dismounted. The Cheyenne braves sat impassively, their weapons at the ready and it occurred to Jubal that this was one of the oddest operations he had ever performed.

The man who had first agreed with Jubal knelt beside him.

'I'm Charley,' he remarked. 'I don't know why the hell you're doin' this, but thanks anyway. Tad an' me can maybe hold him down.'

Jubal grinned. 'Thanks. I'd appreciate that.'

'You sure are one strange cuss,' grunted Tad as he clasped the wounded Jesse by the shoulders.

'Guess I'm just a man of many parts,' said Jubal, 'and being a doctor is one of them.'

He used the scalpel to cut the flesh around the wound so that he would have room to withdraw the arrowhead. He had seen Cheyenne arrows during his stay in their village and knew that the head would most likely be made of chipped stone and difficult to remove. Jesse was half-conscious and Jubal hoped that the pain of withdrawal would not push the man over the borderline into uncontrollable shock.

Probing as gently as he could, he located the arrow's head and inserted a long-handled probe in the wound. Jesse screamed as the instrument went in and Charley and Tad were required to bear down heavily on his shoulders and legs to prevent him from breaking free of Jubal's firm grasp.

Crouched on the groundsheet, the doctor ignored the stream of tobacco-brown spittle that erupted from between Jesse's lips as he pulled the arrowhead free. He applied antiseptic to the wound and then dusted it with sulphur powder before applying a dressing. It was necessary to remove the man's clothing to bandage the hole, but Jubal worked fast to perform his hippocratic duty before the cold took hold.

When he was finished, he pulled Jesse's shirt back over his chest, where the wounded arm was held firmly down by the bandage, and quickly dressed the man again.

He cleaned his instruments, replaced them in the valise and stood up.

'He should be all right now,' he said, 'just ride easy and don't let him use that arm. Keep him warm and feed him well. And when you get back to Denver take him to a doctor there.'

Tad stood up, towering a good four inches over Jubal's slight frame.

'If I hadn't seen it, I wouldn't have believed it,' he said, reluctant admiration showing on his face. 'I had you figgered for a killer an' a renegade. Mebbe I was wrong.'

'Could be,' grinned Jubal as he snapped the medical bag closed and stowed it back on his saddle, 'perhaps there's more to an argument than Marshal Riley's say so.'

'Reckon you could be right, *doc*,' Tad emphasized the last word. 'Reckon I'll talk to Les Riley on the way back.'

'You do that,' said Jubal, 'you might learn some interesting facts.'

He helped Jesse back on to his horse and accepted the hand that the man offered.

'Thanks, doc. Guess you saved my life. I don't know why, but thanks all the same.'

'A pleasure,' grinned Jubal, 'it was just a pity you had to get hurt in the first place.'

'I won't forget,' Jesse assured him. 'I ain't about to go shootin' the man who saved my life again.'

'If you ever see me around town again,' said Jubal, 'I hope you'll remember that promise.'

'Don't worry, doc,' interrupted Charley, 'we all will.'

Les Riley moved his horse up to stand between Jubal and the three buffalo hunters.

'An' don't you forget mine, Cade,' he said coldly. 'Like I said, I'll see you again. Only next time you'll be on the wrong side of a bullet.'

Jubal grinned as he swung into the saddle. 'Marshal,' he said, 'with a peace officer like you around I wonder how the crooks get a look-in.'

Riley snarled and headed his mount down the trail, the three wondering survivors of the posse following at a slower pace. Jubal sat watching them as Little Bear ordered five braves to trail the white men in case they should attempt to double back. Together, they turned their animals in the opposite direction and began the ride to the Cheyenne village. Little Bear broke the silence that had reigned since the whites started back for Denver.

'Friend Jubal,' he said in his broken English, 'you one strange man. First you kill them, then you heal them. Why?'

'Guess a man needs as many friends as he can get, Little Bear. And if you have to hurt them to heal them, I suppose you could say that the mend justifies the pains.'

CHAPTER ELEVEN

Jubal entered the Cheyenne village as dusk was falling, Little Bear escorting him directly to the chief's tepee where Big Wolf sat, quietly smoking a pipe as his wife and daughters bustled about preparing the evening meal. The old Indian relinquished the pipe in favour of one of Jubal's cheroots and indicated that the white man should sit beside him. Little Bear and Satanka joined them to discuss the outcome of Jubal's mission to Denver.

'The Army chief will talk peace,' he began, 'but you must agree a meeting place. Either here or in Denver.'

'No,' grunted Big Wolf, 'if we go to the town we shall be killed by the white eyes. If they find our village they will come here and fight us. It has happened before.'

In the light of recent American history there was no argument Jubal could advance to contradict the chief's statement so he waited for an alternative suggestion.

'We shall meet the horse soldiers where the river runs shallow,' said Big Wolf, 'at the place you call Fisher's Crossing.'

'When?' asked Jubal.

'On the fifth day of the Melting Snow Moon.'

Little Bear stepped in to explain, as best he could, the Cheyenne calendar and Jubal calculated that it would be towards the middle of March, about ten days away.

'I have spoken with Tatanka Iyotake – Sitting Bull in your language – and he agrees,' continued Big Wolf. 'His Sioux will not fight until we have spoken. Unless he is attacked again.'

Satanka broke in. 'If the yellow-hair soldier chief is near,' he said urgently, 'then there will be fighting. He looks for glory and hopes to find it in the bodies of our people.'

'Do you mean Captain Simms, the Denver chief?' asked Jubal.

'No,' replied Satanka, 'there is another, a man called Custer. A killer of women and old men.'

Big Wolf and Little Bear nodded their assent and Jubal realized that he was seeing the other side of the popular picture. He had heard of George Armstrong Custer, the Boy General, during the Civil War. The young man had risen like a military meteor when he had fought for the Union in the War Between The States and ever since his name and picture had cropped up frequently in newspapers and magazines. He was hailed as a dashing young hero, a gallant defender of white civilization against the painted savages who roamed the lands Washington wanted to settle.

'Perhaps,' Jubal thought, 'the Boy General is not quite so gallant as the press makes out.'

The Indians had fallen silent and Jubal spoke quickly, to reassure them.

'I have the word of Captain Simms,' he said, 'that you will not be harmed. He asked me to find you so that I could deliver his message. He does not want to fight you, but to talk with you so that white men and Indians may live in peace.'

'It is good,' said Big Wolf, 'there has been too much fighting. If the soldier chief will take away the buffalo killers and give us the word of the white chief in Washington that we shall be left alone, then there need be no more fighting.' He sighed as his eyes looked out beyond Jubal to a time now past. 'I remember when there were no white men here,' he said in a low, deep voice full of memory, 'when the buffalo ran all day and the Indians lived free under the eyes of the Great Spirit. That time is gone and we must learn new things, but we will not give up our country. That is ours. It does not belong to the white men. We must share some of it with them, but they will not take it all from us.'

His chin sank on to his chest as he fell silent, contemplating the past.

Little Bear began to speak. 'Jubal, we trust you and if you say the soldiers will talk peace then we shall meet them.'

'Good,' Jubal said, not sure how much Simms was empowered to concede but, none the less, pleased that there was at least a chance of saving the Cheyenne from an all-out war.

'I shall return with your message.'

Big Wolf was singing softly to himself and the two younger Indians rose to leave, gesturing that Jubal should accompany them. Together, the three men walked through the camp to the tepee set aside for Jubal. The two Cheyenne entered with him, eager to hear his account of the fight at the frozen lake and to know why the posse had chased him so hard. It was well into the night before the story was finished and Jubal prepared to sleep, his reputation among the Cheyenne grown even bigger as a result of his latest exploits.

He settled himself beneath the buffalo robe and pondered his next move. He would have to return to Denver: he felt a curious duty to the Indians. But the journey would be extremely dangerous. He had no doubts that Riley would live up to his murderous promise and take the first opportunity to kill Jubal. At the same time the buffalo hunters would be after his blood. Consequently an appearance in Denver would almost certainly guarantee his death; he could probably handle Riley, but the overall odds were too heavily weighted against him. His best move, he decided, would be to slip into the Army camp, preferably unseen, and deliver his message direct to Captain Simms. Then he could either hole up in Simms's quarters or head out of town. After the peace talks he could, with help from Simms, get on board the train for St. Louis, the one he had originally intended to catch.

He hunkered down into the warmth of the skin bed, pushed his worries to the back of his mind, and fell asleep.

The smell of cooking woke him the next morning and he emerged from his tepee to find the village fully awake. A circle of smiling children was stationed at the entrance of his tepee, all anxious to catch sight of the strange white man whose fame had spread through the camp. Two boys approached carrying a steaming cauldron of hot water which they set down at the tent flap before scurrying back to join their friends. It was rather unnerving, Jubal thought, to have an audience when you shaved, but the luxury of the hot water after several days on the trail and the frank curiosity of the children prompted him to carry out the morning's ritual as though he were alone.

He was drawing the cut-throat razor over the last remnants of beard growth as Little Bear, accompanied by Satanka, joined him. The war chief barked a guttural command at the children, smiling as they scattered away from Jubal's tepee, and squatted down at the entrance.

'You go today?' he asked.

'I guess so,' Jubal nodded. 'It'll take me three or four days to get back and at least one more for the Army man to organize the meeting. Allow two more for him to ride to the crossing, maybe more if he brings a column.'

'Why he bring soldiers?' demanded Satanka.

'It's the Army way,' grinned Jubal, wiping his face free of shaving soap. 'No soldier ever went to a peace conference without at least one troop to back him up.'

'Indians take one man's word,' grunted the Cheyenne medicine man, 'why not the white men? They do not trust one another?'

'You better believe it,' said Jubal. 'The more people you got to witness something, the better chance you got of making it stick.'

The two Indians nodded agreement.

'Then we bring Dog Soldiers,' Little Bear announced firmly, 'all watch: treaty kept.'

'I hope so,' said Jubal, 'for all concerned.'

He rubbed a hand over his protesting stomach and inquired about food. The two Cheyenne led him over to Little Bear's lodge, where the Indian's wife had prepared a meal. Jubal ate hungrily, using his fingers to pluck chunks of steaming meat from the cooking pot hung over a small fire. When he had finished he asked Little Bear about horses. The Cheyenne told him that his own mount had been fed and watered and now awaited Jubal.

'Then I'd better get going,' he remarked.

'We ride with you to the crossing,' said the Cheyenne. 'If white men try to ambush you we kill them.'

'Thanks,' grinned Jubal, 'but try not to kill anyone. It's not the best way to start peace talks.'

He grinned tightly at the irony of his words. As a messenger on a peace mission he had not got off to the best possible start. But then, he mused, there could not be too many messengers of peace with a bounty on their head and a killer marshal on their tail.

'Do not worry, Jubal,' said Satanka, 'we only kill if we have to. Indians are not like white men.'

'You're right there,' grinned Jubal in reply. 'I just wish a few more white men thought the same way.'

He returned to his tepee to collect his rifle and medical bag and then, accompanied by Satanka and Little Bear, went to pay his respects to Big Wolf. The old chief had recovered from the melancholy of the previous night and wished Jubal a safe and successful trip. He would stay in the village until it was time to leave for the meeting, using the interim period to send messages to the Sioux camped north of the village to tell them of the latest developments and urge them again to curb their warlike instincts until Jubal had organized the peace talks.

He walked with Jubal to the waiting horses, watching as the small white man swung up into the saddle.

Then he raised his hand in a gesture that was half farewell and half a blessing.

'I have heard,' he said loud enough so that all the escort could hear, 'of a white man raised by another Cheyenne village. They call him Little Big Man. I think we have our own Little Big Man now. We shall remember you, Jubal.'

'Thanks,' smiled Jubal, 'maybe someday someone will write a book about me.'

CHAPTER TWELVE

They rode back along the snow-covered trail to the lake. The ice broken by Jubal's gunfire and the pounding of the horses' hooves was beginning to re-form, although it was obvious that spring was not far off. The trail was easier to follow as there had been no fresh snowfall and the weather was distinctly warmer than it had been the last time Jubal rode towards Denver. They did not push their mounts hard as Jubal had been forced to do on the way in to the camp and decided to spend the night on the lake shore.

Blankets were stretched over tree branches to make temporary shelters and fires started for the evening meal. Once again Jubal was called upon to tell the story of his fight and the Cheyenne warriors laughed their appreciation of his account, eyeing the broken ice wonderingly. Irrespective of the outcome of the peace talks, they enjoyed a good story, especially one that concerned a battle against heavy odds.

The next day they pushed on through the thawing snow in the direction of Fisher's Crossing, breaking the journey to run down a deer that was careless enough to wander across their path.

That night they ate well, making camp just north of the ford. The horse Jubal had left there was gone, but the grain he had dropped was eaten and one of the Cheyenne claimed to make out tracks leading back to the crossing. Jubal hoped the animal had managed to get back to its corral.

In the morning the main band of warriors broke off to return to their village, leaving Little Bear, Satanka and three others to continue on the trail.

They rode for two more days, taking an easy pace with three Cheyenne always in front to scout the terrain should Riley have left an ambush party to wait for Jubal. But there was no sign of attack and on the morning of the third day they came in sight of Denver. There the Indians left Jubal to go in alone. They headed back the way they had come, promising to meet at the crossing on the Platte in five days' time.

Jubal found a sheltered spot along the river bank and settled down to wait for nightfall before riding in to the Army bivouac in search of Captain Simms.

It was full dark before he risked moving and the glow of Denver's lights outlined the town against the sky. A full moon threw long shadows across the snow, producing an eerie effect as it illuminated drift-heads with a cold, clear brilliance that was translated into stark black on the far sides of the hummocks. Jubal moved forwards slowly, picking his way with infinite care so that his horse did not stumble as it trod gingerly over the freezing snow. Where loose drifts had previously lain there were now patches of ice, melted during the day by the spring thaw and frozen come nightfall by the dramatic lowering of the temperature. Midnight was not far off when Jubal came up to the outskirts of the Army camp and dismounted.

He ground-hitched the horse and draped a blanket over its back. Later, he hoped to send someone to collect it, but right now he wanted to get inside the bivouac and speak with Simms.

Stealthily, he slipped into the circle of tents, listening intently for the sound of an approaching sentry. He was passing through the third circle before he was challenged.

'What the hell?' the voice came from a young trooper emerging from the entrance of a one-man pup tent. 'Who are you?'

Jubal stood upright in one clean movement, swinging the stock of the Spencer up level with the soldier's jaw. It connected with a dull thud that snapped the man's head back as his eyes closed on an explosion of coloured light. His knees buckled and he slumped to the ground. Jubal caught the falling body before it measured its length on the snow and dragged the unconscious trooper back inside his tent.

'Sorry, friend,' he muttered under his breath, 'but I just can't afford to take any chances.'

He laid the soldier inside the tent, closed the flap and continued in the direction of the headquarters building.

The hut was guarded by two armed troopers and Jubal lay prone, considering the best approach. He began to worm his way across the frozen ground, heading for the rear of the building where he remembered a window opened into the captain's sleeping quarters. He covered the distance to the hut unnoticed and peered through the misted glass pane. There was a light showing from the front office, but no sign of anyone in the back room. Cautiously, he tried the window, breathing a sigh of relief when he found it was unfastened. As quietly as he could, he slid the frame upwards and then swung himself over the sill. He slipped to the plank floor and drew the window closed behind him, then cat-footed his way across the room to the door. There was no keyhole so he was forced to listen for several long moments before he was sure that the outer room contained only one man. When he was certain he pushed the door open with the barrel of the Spencer and, the rifle held ready before him, stepped into the room.

Captain Simms looked up from his desk as the door flew open.

'Cade!' he cried, surprise mingling with relief, 'I thought you were dead. Your horse came back and then Les Riley turned up with some story of the Indians picking you up.'

'It's a long tale, Captain,' Jubal grinned, 'and better told over hot coffee. You mind?' he gestured at the coffee-pot on the stove.

'Of course not,' Simms shook his head, 'help yourself.'

Jubal poured a cup, removed his coat and began to talk. He told Simms of Marshal Riley's pursuit and the fight with the posse, of his meeting with the Cheyenne and the removal of the arrow from Jesse's shoulder. Then he went on to tell the Army man of Big Wolf's promise to meet and the old chief's desire for peace.

'Good,' murmured Simms when the story was ended, 'we'll meet the Cheyenne at the crossing. You'd better stay out of sight until then: Riley's gunning for you.'

'What's the story?' Jubal wondered. 'Am I still wanted?'

'Riley wants you,' said Simms, 'badly. And there are quite

a few buffalo hunters would be happy to kill you. But that patch-up job you did on Jesse has convinced a good few of them that you're not all bad. Jesse told them about the fight at the lake and there's a good number of townsfolk reckon you were in the right. They're about as sick of the hunters as I am. Riley was all for posting a reward on you, but I managed to talk the city authorities out of that. At least until it's decided by the circuit judge, and he won't be around for a month at least. With any luck you'll be gone by then and if you are posted you'll only be wanted in Colorado. The jurisdiction won't stretch any farther. Your main problem is Riley.'

'Yeah,' Jubal agreed, 'the marshal's smelled money and he won't give it up easily.'

'Damn' right,' Simms nodded his assent. 'The marshal wants that bounty and I don't believe he cares too much how he gets it.'

'Let's hope he doesn't,' grinned Jubal, 'I've got better things to do than supply a crooked lawman with a pension.'

He yawned widely and stretched his arms.

'If you don't mind, Captain, I think I'd better stay here until the meeting.'

Simms agreed, ushering Jubal into the back room where a bed was made up. Jubal could stay there, Simms told him, while the captain would spend the next few nights in town. It was not so unusual as to arouse suspicion among his men and would give him a chance to sound out feelings around the place. Jubal accepted the offer gratefully and settled down to sleep.

The next few days proved excruciatingly boring. Jubal was by nature an active man and the enforced confinement – albeit necessary – grated on his nerves. Captain Simms was occupied most of the time by military duties, so that Jubal had few chances to talk with him and he saw no other person. Simms arranged to bring him food from the commissary and laid in a supply of cheroots. Jubal spent most of his time re-reading the few medical books he carried with him and studying the captain's military tomes. He sometimes wondered if visitors to the hut would not spot the odour of cigar smoke that filled the place after his first two days in hiding, but trusted to the captain's ingenuity to explain away the smell. By the time Simms was ready to start out for the meeting with the Cheyenne, Jubal felt that he could sit a military exam – and wondered if he would ever want to smoke again.

Simms had planned the expedition's start for daybreak to avoid an excess of sightseers who might recognize Jubal. He had picked up no new information about Riley's activities and was fairly confident that the incident of the jail break and the chase had been forgotten by most of the men concerned, with Riley making the most notable – and dangerous – exception. Jubal was less confident but could see no alternative to risking the trip north. In any event, he was glad to get back out into the fresh air.

It was a clear, cold morning that carried a strong hint of better weather to come and Jubal suspected that Big Wolf had chosen the time deliberately. The day felt as though winter was over and the people of the High Plains could look forward to more cheerful weather. Certainly, the troopers of the Denver garrison seemed in better spirits, the men detailed to accompany Simms showing excitement at the prospect of a break in the monotony of camp life.

They rode out in good order, several cavalrymen wondering loudly at the small figure huddled in an Army greatcoat that rode alongside the captain.

Simms had formed two troops in front of his headquarters, the mounted men drawn up in ranks that effectively blocked the building from casual view so that Jubal, wearing the borrowed greatcoat, was able to slip almost unseen from the hut and mount the horse Simms had provided. A woollen muffler hid most of his face and the only distinguishing mark was the grey derby that he still wore on his black hair.

If any of the captain's hand-picked troopers did recognize him, they kept silent, giving Jubal cause to be grateful for military discipline.

After the squadron had pitched camp for the night Simms made Jubal's presence officially known. He called the men into a group around the central fire and delivered a short speech itemizing the events of the past few weeks and explaining

Jubal's part in them. A grizzled sergeant spoke up for the assembled troopers.

'I never did have too much time for buffler killers,' he took a swig from the mug in his hand before going on, 'an' I heard about the fight in the saloon. Seems to me the doc shouldn't have been thrown in the pokey in the first place. So if he got out I can't hardly blame him an' if I had a pack of gun-happy boyos on my tail I reckon I'd do much the same thing.'

The soldiers around him murmured their agreement.

'So I reckon,' the sergeant continued, 'that it ain't like he done anythin' illegal. He was just lookin' after hisself like anyone's got a right to do.'

'Good fer you, doc.' It was a voice from the back of the crowd and it was taken up by others.

'Well, Cade,' Simms smiled, 'it looks as though the cavalry has adopted you.'

They turned in for the night, several soldiers stepping forward to assure Jubal of their support in the event of trouble before retiring to their bedrolls. He hoped the coming talks would justify their optimism.

CHAPTER THIRTEEN

In the late afternoon of the third day out of Denver the column reached Fisher's Crossing. There was no sign of the Cheyenne so Captain Simms ordered his men to pitch camp on the river bank to await the arrival of Big Wolf and his people. Tents were swiftly erected, the horses tethered by the sleeping quarters of their riders and picket lines set up. Everything was done with tidy military efficiency and the last few tents were going up as the first fires blazed into life. The troopers detailed for kitchen duty began to prepare the evening meal and an appetizing smell soon filled the air.

Mixed with the cheerful bustle of the camp was an air of expectancy. Men kept their guns close at hand and strayed no farther from their horses than they had to. For all the optimism of the venture, the Army was taking no chances on a surprise attack. Jubal wondered how much was due to experience of Indian fighting and how much to the white men's built-in fear of the 'hostiles', an apprehension fuelled by the popular press and the fact – if the troopers were honest with themselves – that they were, effectively, trespassing upon the traditional hunting grounds of the Plains tribes.

For all the tension, however, the night passed quietly and the pale morning sun showed nothing more than a fresh fall of snow.

Captain Simms spent the morning organizing the setting for the parley. He detailed troopers to erect a large, open tent on the river bank, its interior in clear view of both the Army bivouac and the far side of the Platte. Inside, he had folding camp-chairs and a wood table set up, a small metal trunk in the centre of the table containing the hurriedly prepared terms drafted by the Army.

The chairs were being re-arranged for the second time when the first Cheyenne appeared. Jubal recognized Little

Bear instantly and raised a hand in greeting. The war chief sat his pony on the opposite bank, a long-tailed eagle feather bonnet trailing along its flanks. He was wearing a brightly coloured buckskin shirt and fringed leggings, a tomahawk was tucked into his beaded belt and he carried a lance, with two black-tipped feathers tied to its head, in his right hand. He lifted the weapon in reply to Jubal's wave and shouted back over his shoulder. In an order that matched the Cavalry's own discipline, two ranks of Dog Soldiers appeared behind him, armed mostly with bows and lances, but showing, too, an occasional single-shot carbine. The Indians drew up in neat lines facing the whites, then swung tidily into a double lane down which rode Big Wolf and Satanka, three lesser chiefs at their back.

Simms shouted an order as he ran for his horse and the cavalrymen swung into their saddles. They formed a double line to match the Cheyenne so that Big Wolf and his entourage came into the bivouac down a long lane of fighting men.

The old chief could not conceal his pleasure at the pomp of the ceremonial entry and his lined face creased into a broad smile as he approached Simms and Jubal, waiting at the end of the mounted men.

'The Little Big Man speaks true,' he cried as he came up to the parley tent, 'he promised us peace talks and brings the pony soldiers to speak with us. So, let us talk of peace.'

'Nothing would please me more,' replied Captain Simms, 'than to talk peace with the chief of the Cheyenne.'

He called for a trooper to take Big Wolf's pony as the chief dismounted and then stood back to allow the Indian to enter the tent before him. Satanka and Little Bear followed, the latter pausing to speak with Jubal.

'It is good, friend,' he said softly. 'Sitting Bull and his Sioux are ready for a war. It would be a bad thing for everyone. Better that we talk peace now before your people fill the Paha Sapa – the Black Hills, you call them – and we are forced to fight.'

'I hope so,' replied Jubal, 'wars never did anyone much good.'

'Better peace between friends,' murmured Little Bear, 'than

a piece of enemy ground.'

They joined the group sitting under the spread canvas as Simms began a speech of formal welcome. He expressed, on behalf of his commanding officer and the War Department in Washington, their pleasure that Big Wolf and his tribe were willing to come in for the parley. The Cheyenne leader replied in kind, emphasizing his desire for an amicable settlement of the hostilities and the wish of the Plains Indians to be left alone to continue their traditional way of life, without interference from white invaders. He spoke of the Indians' desire to live in peace under the will of the Great White Father, and their acceptance of the white man's need to cross the hunting grounds – so long as settlers and miners and railways were kept out of the Plains.

'It is our land,' he said, 'and it has always been our land. We have lived with the buffalo and the grass and the forests since before the white men came here. Now they are here and we must share the land. This we will do. And we will live in peace so long as the white men do not try to take the land from us.'

The reply was somewhat hampered by the official view Simms was forced to put forward and Jubal could see that the talks would take some time. He listened to the young Army officer and the old Cheyenne exchanging views, official and personal, as the sun began to set behind the rolling snow fields. They went on talking until it was close to full dark and they decided to continue in the morning. The Cheyenne departed for their camp across the river and the Army settled down for the night.

Fifteen miles back towards Denver, Marshal Les Riley and sixty buffalo hunters were pitching camp. They kept their fires small so that no glow would give away their position on the flat, snowbound plain. They ate strips of cold pemmican as they huddled into their coats, pulling blankets around their shoulders against the cold. Riley and a few others carried Winchester rifles, but most of the group were armed with the basic tool of their trade: the Sharps ·50 calibre buffalo gun.

They were armed equally with their hate of anything to do with the Indians and their fear that the buffalo trade might come to an end. Riley nursed his desire to kill Jubal and claim Agnew's bounty. The others chewed over Riley's promise that Jubal and Simms would make a peace treaty that would end their way of life.

And every one of them was determined to wipe out the threat.

They broke camp at sun-up and rode cautiously in the direction of Fisher's Crossing.

North of the advancing column, Simms and Big Wolf had begun their talks for the second day. The Cheyenne chief had ridden into the camp as breakfast was started and had expressed his delight in the white man's drink called coffee. He had refused to talk until six cups were drunk and then, satisfied with the rare luxury, had joined Simms in the parley tent.

The talks were going well, both parties willing to listen to the other's point of view and both sympathetic to the difficulties of speaking for a whole nation. Big Wolf expressed his understanding of the white man's need to travel through to the Californian coast while Captain Simms showed a degree of diplomacy that surprised Jubal as he conceded the Indians' need to retain their hunting grounds without being contained on reservations. Perhaps, mused Jubal as he listened to the talk flowing back and forth across the table, this could mean the beginning of something new. A time of peace, when red and white men might live together in harmony, without the constant, smouldering warfare that had dogged the Plains for so long. Perhaps his unexpected encounter with Little Bear might have a long-lasting effect.

His thoughts were interrupted by a high-pitched scream. As he powered himself up out of the canvas chair he saw a trooper pitch forwards on to his face, blood spreading redly across the thick blue cloth of his winter coat. The soldier clawed painfully at the stained snow as the echo of the killing shot rang out over the plain.

Big Wolf and his sub-chiefs were out of their seats at the same time, Little Bear shouting for his Dog Soldiers as his chief glared at Captain Simms.

'What happens?' he roared. 'White man's treachery?'

102

Jubal intervened. 'That's a white soldier on the ground.'

'Dammit, Big Wolf,' it was Simms, shouting above the roar of confusion that swept the camp as cavalrymen and Cheyenne raced for their horses, 'I didn't bring you here to kill you. And it's one of my men dead. Look to your own braves.'

A second shot boomed across the snow. This time a Cheyenne, swinging on to his pony, threw up his arms and sprawled on to the ground.

'Hell!' Jubal yelled, 'I know that sound. It's a buffalo gun.'

'You're right,' Simms shouted back, 'but what the devil's happening?'

A third shot spread flakes of snow from the tent's roof over their faces as a neat, round hole appeared in the canvas. Jubal had his Spencer in his hands, hammer cocked ready to fire.

'I'm not sure,' he grated through clenched teeth, 'but at a rough guess I'd say that Riley's found me.'

He put his own body in front of the Cheyenne chief as Big Wolf ran towards his pony. Little Bear and Satanka were already mounted, their weapons ready to fire upon the soldiers running for their own horses. Jubal called out as he swung on to his own animal.

'Little Bear! Don't shoot. It's not the pony soldiers.'

He spun the horse around, smashing his heels hard into its ribs, hoping that the others would follow. They did, the Cheyenne war chief galloping up alongside.

'Who then?' he shouted. 'Who does fire?'

'Buffalo hunters,' Jubal bellowed, 'they must have trailed us. They want to stop the talks.'

'Then we stop them,' grunted Little Bear, heeling his pony ahead of Jubal's weightier animal, 'dead.'

Captain Simms was shouting orders to his men as the Dog Soldiers thundered out of the camp. He broke off as Jubal raced past him.

'Cade,' he bellowed, 'hold those Indians in check. Wait for me.'

Jubal had little choice in the matter. The Cheyenne warriors had come in to talk peace and now they wanted to know who was responsible for the unexpected attack. He yelled an unintelligible reply to the angry soldier, wheeling his horse to match Little Bear's swing around the circle of tents. Big Wolf, looking as though he would enjoy the fight even more than the talks, had come up alongside, and the three men, two Indians flanking Jubal, raced towards the source of the attack.

There was a volley of bullets that whistled past them, lifting several of the following Indians from their rawhide saddles but somehow missing the lead trio. Jubal could see dark figures outlined against the snow a good quarter-mile ahead, and wondered how the Cheyenne hoped to reach them alive. Beside him, Little Bear and Big Wolf did not seem to entertain any such doubts as they spurred their ponies onwards, screaming war cries. Suddenly, they swung their ponies off to one side, racing down the gently sloping bank of the river, so that their passage was temporarily hidden from the attackers' view. They galloped on as Jubal realized that the charge was calculated with far more care than he had thought: if they continued along the river they would end up on the buffalo hunters' flank in a good position to mount a counter-attack.

He glanced at the grimly smiling Cheyenne on either side of him, his own face twisting into the rictus of hate that gripped him at such moments.

Although he had not spotted Riley, he was sure that it was the marshal who had prompted the attack and the thought of the man going to such lengths to secure Agnew's bounty stretched the skin tight across his cheekbones as his nostrils flared in fury. He steered his horse with one hand, the other holding the Spencer ready to fire.

Behind him, Jubal heard the shrilling of a bugle as Simms led his troopers into a charge. Unlike the Cheyenne, the soldiers attacked in text-book formation. They spread out into a skirmish line as they ploughed through the snow, head on towards the ambushers. Even over the thunder of hooves on hard-packed snow, he could hear the screams of wounded horses and men as the booming of heavy calibre rifles tore at the air.

There were only twenty men riding with Captain Simms

and fifteen of the Cheyenne Dog Soldiers, but the speed of the Indians' counter-attack went in their favour.

The yelling riders boiled over the edge of the river bank as they came alongside the hunters' position. Bows hummed as arrows sped towards swiftly sighted targets and Jubal wrapped his reins around his saddle horn to allow free movement of the Spencer. Firing from the hip, he put a bullet through the chest of a buffalo hunter who was bringing his Sharps to bear on the Indians. The man threw up his arms, the gun flying high into the air as he toppled backwards, blood spuming from his chest.

Jubal saw several more fall with arrows sprouting like pine needles from their heavy coats and then he was in among them. Beside him, Big Wolf swung a hatchet in a savage over-hand blow that split a man's skull like a cloven melon. The hunter stood, his rifle still clutched in senseless fingers, as blood and brain matter dribbled down his face. Then he buckled at the knees and fell sideways, toppling the man beside him so that he was thrown into the path of a charging pony. The hooves crashed down on to his chest and he screamed as his ribs broke under the impact, white splinters of bone suddenly appearing through his shirt.

Then they were through and wheeling around to attack again. But Simms and his troopers were there first. Sabres flashed in the wan sunlight as the cavalry smashed through the ranks of suddenly demoralized buffalo men. The swords rose, red-edged now as men clutched at severed limbs and gashed faces. At his side, Jubal heard a yell of glee.

'A good fight.' It was Little Bear, a lance held in his right hand. 'The pony soldiers fight well.'

'So let's go help them,' Jubal shouted back, levering a fresh shell into the breech of the Spencer.

Little Bear needed no more prompting and pushed his pony into a furious gallop at the centre of the battle. Simms and his men had ridden clear on the far side of the ambush and were regrouping for a second charge as the Cheyenne hit again. Jubal blew away a man's face as the wave of horsemen washed over the buffalo hunters, levered the Spencer and fired pointblank at a bearded man who was desperately thumbing a cartridge into the loading gate of a smoking rifle. He spat blood out over his beard and cursed as the ·30 calibre shell ploughed a ragged hole through his stomach. Then, clutching at the wound, he doubled over, his legs kicking madly as he died.

Little Bear swung his pony around so that its hindquarters careened into another rifleman, knocking him flying, and without pausing levelled his lance on a running figure directly in his path. The stone tip went in under the man's right shoulder blade, emerging from his lower ribcage in a welter of scarlet blood as he was lifted off his feet and carried forwards by the impetus of the thrust. With a practised movement, the Cheyenne twisted the lance clear, allowing the body to tumble lifeless in front of the charging ponies.

Jubal crouched in his saddle as a bullet singed his neck and rammed the Spencer, muzzle first, into the face of the would-be killer. The metal smashed deep into the mouth, pulping lips against teeth which broke under the impact, hurling the man backwards, off balance as he clutched at his ruined mouth. A warrior riding close behind Jubal swung a tomahawk that finished Jubal's work, cutting savagely into the man's neck, so that his head swung lopsided and bathed in blood as he crumpled on to the tainted snow.

'Wait!' Jubal yelled as they reached the river and turned for a third charge. 'Let the pony soldiers go through.'

'Enough for everyone,' replied Little Bear, signalling to his braves to hold back.

Captain Simms led his cavalry into their second rush in good order. Carbines barked as the blue-clad figures hurtled onwards, then were sheathed in favour of naked steel. Again Jubal watched the sabres rise and fall among the buffalo hunters, heard the screams of dying men, clearer now that he was no longer in their midst, and grinned fiercely at the carnage spread before him. The Cheyenne braves were supporting the troopers with a deadly rain of arrows, picking off ambushers who had survived the first charges so that the hunters were reduced to a fraction of their original numbers. Jubal triggered the Spencer as though he was on a shooting range, picking his targets with calm deliberation and dropping

106

them like so many clay pigeons. He paused only to push fresh shells into the rifle before bringing it back up to his shoulder and firing again. By the time the cavalry had ridden clear of the milling figures Riley's men were reduced to a handful of bloody, bewildered survivors.

Throughout the fight, Jubal had not seen the marshal and now he scanned the battleground for sight of the moustached peace officer. He spotted him as Riley appeared suddenly on horseback, driving the buffalo hunters' animals before him. The lawman had tied a blanket to a horse's tail and fired the material to spook the beast so that it galloped forwards in a futile attempt to escape the flames licking at its hindquarters.

Around the fear-crazed animal thundered the other horses, racing towards the river where the Cheyenne were grouped, downstream from the panting soldiers. They scattered as the better part of fifty maddened animals flew straight at them and Jubal found his aim obscured by the cascading snow thrown up by the pounding hooves. He turned his own mount to one side in an attempt to avoid the crushing impact of the stampeding herd and joined soldiers and Indians in a desperate race for safety. The unlikely allies headed north and south along the river as the racing horses pounded into the water. Icy spray was thrown high, raining down over cursing cavalrymen and whooping braves, as the animals hit the Platte. The freezing water doused the blazing material of the blanket, but the horses, still driven by their fear, ploughed on up the opposite bank to disappear into the trees.

Jubal pushed his own horse up to the rim of the river bank and caught sight of the few remaining ambushers riding hard in the direction of Denver. He realized that there was little point in going after them: his animal was winded from the fierce rushes of the battle while Riley and his men, having fought on foot, were riding fresh ponies.

'Like you said one time, Riley,' he muttered to himself, 'I'll see you again.'

'And when you do?' It was Simms. 'What will you do?'

'Kill him,' Jubal said bleakly.

'Just hope I don't get to him first,' snarled the soldier, 'because if I do he's dead.'

'First come, first served, I guess,' Jubal answered. 'Either way I'd like to see his corpse.'

'Plenty on the ice,' Little Bear, flanked by Big Wolf and Satanka, had joined them. 'We fight good together.'

Jubal grinned at the smiling Cheyenne, then noticed blood running down his leg, staining the buckskin a dark brown.

'You hurt?' he asked.

'Nothing bad,' replied Little Bear, 'only a wounded knee.'

'I guess that won't bury you,' grinned Jubal.

CHAPTER FOURTEEN

Four troopers were dead and eight Cheyenne, but the speed and ferocity of the counter-attack had taken the buffalo hunters by surprise. The better part of the gang was stretched on the snow with the surviving Indians stripping the bodies of weapons. Captain Simms allowed it to go on as his men prepared the dead soldiers for burial, although, by tacit agreement with Big Wolf, no scalps were taken. Jubal and Satanka moved among the wounded, dressing bullet holes and splinting broken bones. There was no more talk of peace, just a grim silence that settled over the figures on the windswept plain, broken only by the cries of the wounded and, occasionally, the low murmur of a reassuring voice as a trooper comforted a hurt comrade.

Jubal finished bandaging a ragged gash that ran down the arm of a Cheyenne brave and went in search of Little Bear. He found the war chief standing beside his pony, watching as his Dog Soldiers wrapped their dead in buffalo skin robes prior to their return to the village and the ceremonial funeral rites that would follow.

'I guess there's not much to say,' Jubal murmured, 'but I'm sorry.'

'You tried to make peace,' replied the Cheyenne, 'that is good. You and the soldier chief speak straight. The Cheyenne can trust you. It is the others who make war. They want our land and our buffalo and they will kill us to take it. It is sad that they are many and the good whites are few because we will not give them the land, and they will not take it easily. We shall fight if we must and many men will die.'

'It is as Sitting Bull says,' Big Wolf had come to join them. 'If the white men leave us alone then we can live in peace. If they will not, there will be war.'

They went over to Simms who was directing his men as

they struck camp. The soldier looked both angry and disappointed and was clearly embarrassed at the violent outcome of his peace mission. He apologized to the two Indians in a final attempt to salvage something from the mess, assuring them that when he returned to Denver he would personally see to it that the surviving ambushers were punished. Big Wolf placed a gnarled hand on the younger man's shoulder.

'Like Jubal,' he said, 'you speak straight and now the Cheyenne will listen to your words, and know they are true. But your voice is not the voice of all white men. When you speak for all your people come back and we will talk. But now we shall go north to where the Sioux are camped. The land is good in the Greasy Grass country, the place you call the Little Big Horn. We can live in peace there because we are many and the white men few. I will speak with Sitting Bull and tell him of your words. But you must go back and tell the White Soldier Chief that we shall fight if we must.'

He turned away and climbed on to his pony.

'Go in peace, Jubal,' he said, gathering the single strand of the rawhide bridle in his left hand, 'and know that where the Cheyenne are, there you will ride among brothers.'

Jubal raised a hand in silent farewell as Big Wolf barked a command to his warriors and led them back across the Platte. Little Bear and Satanka followed him, both Indians raising their weapons in salute as they went past. He watched the Cheyenne splash through the river and disappear among the trees on the far side.

'Damn,' said Simms disgustedly, 'by the time this gets around there won't be an Indian on the Plains willing to talk peace. Next thing we know there'll be a full-scale war.'

'At least we tried,' replied Jubal.

'Yeah. And now let's head back to town and try Riley.'

'You think he'll still be in town?' asked Jubal.

Simms shrugged. 'I don't know. But if he is I want him in jail. He could get away with shooting Indians, but killing United States soldiers is another matter.'

As they rode away from Fisher's Crossing a wolf appeared from among the pines. Padding soft and swift over the white ground, the beast approached the corpses of the buffalo

110

hunters, left where they had fallen in the fight. Warily, it eyed the retreating column of mounted men then, confident that it could feast undisturbed, it threw back its head and howled. From among the trees dark shapes loped forwards, yellow fangs grinning in the sunlight. Jubal looked back as the wolf pack began to feed and a tight, humourless grin creased his lips.

Around the area of the fight bright, fresh blood spilled over the already-stained snow.

Behind Jubal a soldier laughed cynically. 'Leastways they ain't gonna litter the place.'

'Murdering bastards,' another called back, then raised his voice. 'Good eatin'!'

The wolves ignored them: fresh meat was hard to find in winter.

There was little said on the long ride back. The cavalrymen seemed subdued by the unexpected violence of the fight and the killing of their comrades. What talk went on around the campfires was mostly of revenge and whether the remaining ambushers would still be in Denver, or fled. Jubal felt that the handful of men he had seen riding away would most likely quit the town rather than risk their necks waiting for a troop of angry soldiers eager to stretch them. Marshal Riley, however, was another matter. The lawman had shown how far he was prepared to go in his attempts to kill Jubal and the young doctor was pretty sure that Riley would wait for his return and make at least one more try for the bounty money. This time, though, Jubal would be expecting him.

They got into Denver near dusk and Simms ordered his men to their quarters for fear of a riot. Before he unleashed his angry troopers on the buffalo men he wanted to gauge the feeling of the town. It was not long in making itself known. A group of local dignitaries appeared in the headquarters hut as the captain and Jubal were stowing their gear; they were followed by a crowd of troopers whose hostile eyes watched them enter the building, their voices carrying through the wooden walls in a low, disgruntled murmur. The men were clearly ill at ease, their glances going anywhere other than the two cold, waiting faces confronting them, their hands, muffled in heavy woollen gloves, turning hat brims nervously.

Simms was the first to speak. 'Well? You want something or did you plan on just standing there?'

The oldest man replied. 'No need to take that tone, Captain. We ...'

He broke off as Simms interrupted.

'The hell there's not! Four of my men are dead. Murdered. And there's a dozen wounded. I reckon that gives me the right to take any damn' tone I like. And ask what you plan to do about the killers.'

'I was trying to tell you,' continued the white-bearded man, 'that we came to apologize.'

'There's a bunch of men waiting outside,' snarled the cavalry officer, 'how'd you like to go *apologize* to them? They want to know who did it. Then they want to see them stand trial.' He slapped his gauntlets on the table. 'So do I.'

'We're trying to tell you,' the oldster continued, plucking at his frayed hat brim, 'that the townsfolk had nothing to do with it. It was Riley and the buffalo hunters.'

'Where is Riley?' It was Jubal, his soft voice carrying more emphasis than the heated tones of the others. 'Where did he go?'

The spokesman shuffled his feet. 'Don't rightly know, mister. He raised a posse 'bout a day after you and the captain rode out. There was a lot of talk about renegades and mealy-mouth treaties with the injuns, then they headed after you. Only about six came back an' we haven't seen Riley since.' He paused before adding, 'He ain't the marshal no more. We voted him out of office.'

'Good,' rasped Simms, 'that saves me the trouble of hanging a peace officer.'

'Hey now, Captain,' the speaker was even more worried, 'who's talking about a hanging?'

'I am. On behalf of the United States Cavalry. Those gun-happy bastards may get away with slaughtering Indians but they don't – I repeat: they do not – get away with killing my soldiers.'

Boot heels shifted on the creaking boards as embarrassed eyes studied the knotted wood with more care than it merited,

112

then a sigh of corporate resignation blew the snowflakes dropped from clothing and footwear.

'Guess you're right, Captain. What they did was pretty bad.'

'Bad!' Simms was near boiling point, his fury kept under control only by a strength of will that shook his body like a volcano building up to its ultimate eruption. 'You bet your sweet damn' lives it was bad! It was murder. Wanton, wholesale murder that's likely to push us into a full-scale Indian war. Those Cheyenne are going straight back to the Sioux and tell them about the way white men shoot up peaceful Indians come in for talks. Next damn' thing you know, there's a few thousand redskins on the warpath. That's how bad it was.' He sucked air into his lungs, refuelling his anger. 'And who ends up fighting them? The cavalry, that's who. The friends of the men who got killed.'

'Well, like you say,' the old man went on uneasily, 'it was bad trouble and we figgered the culprits should be punished.' He halted as he sought simultaneously to change his tack and pacify the irate soldier. 'So we checked on the ones who came back. Since we don't have a town marshal right now, I guess – we guess,' he corrected himself, 'that a military trial would be in order.'

'I had something of the kind in mind,' grunted Simms, 'the alternative being that my troopers locate the men themselves and handle the affair.'

The representatives of Denver shifted awkwardly.

'We don't want nothin' like that,' muttered one of them; 'that could mean real bad trouble. You find Jeb Sharkey, he'll tell you who the others were.'

'Jeb Sharkey?' Simms wrote quickly on a pad of note paper. 'He was one of them?'

'Yessir. He was one.'

'But you don't know where Riley is?' Jubal asked again. 'No one's seen him?'

'Nossir.' Whatever dignity the civic authorities had carried into the small, cold hut with them had evaporated under the heat of anger displayed by the two men there and the crowd

113

waiting outside. 'Riley's gone off the face of the earth as far as we can make out.'

'Maybe Sharkey can tell us where,' Simms said coldly. 'We'll find out soon.'

CHAPTER FIFTEEN

Jeb Sharkey was tougher than he looked. It took two cavalry-men to hold him while three more, working in relays, pounded the information out of his broken body. Jubal watched as they went to work against the bar of the Buffalo Horn saloon, two men pinning the hunter's arms down on the long pine table as the others smashed fists and vicious boot caps into his body. By the time they had finished Sharkey was barely capable of speaking, but cold water and more punches drew five names from between his pulped lips.

Two troopers were told off to guard the man while the others went looking for his companions.

They found two in a saloon up Denver's long mainstreet and the other three in a second drinking palace just off the main drag. There, a sympathetic buffalo hunter made the mis-take of pulling a pistol on the group of blue-legs bearing down on his drinking companions.

Jubal was carrying the Spencer, a shell in the breech ready for trouble, which came up as the man rose from his seat. His Colt Dragoon was halfway out of the holster when Jubal's bullet took him under the chin, smashing through his wind-pipe in a great, backward-pouring fountain of red. The un-fired gun slid back into the leather as he toppled over, thrown by the impact of the rifle on to the stained floor, his hands clutching at the sudden hole in his neck.

For long moments Jubal, Simms and the cavalrymen eyed the men seated around the saloon. Cavalry Colts were cocked ready to fire as the blue-coated troopers watched the stinking hunters with hungry eyes. Like wolves waiting for the final kill they stood, each man lusting for the chance to trigger his gun and begin the killing.

Then Simms broke the tension.

'Get them. Sharkey gave us the names – they're the ones

we want. No one else. Just them.'

Squealing like stuck pigs the buffalo hunters were dragged from the saloon and booted down the street to where the first was waiting.

Simms detailed six troopers to bring up their horses and unship their lariats. Jubal watched as the soldiers pulled the neatly tied ropes from their saddles and, on their captain's orders, threw them over the balcony rail of the saloon.

'These men,' Simms shouted for the benefit of the crowd that had gathered to watch the hanging, 'killed soldiers of the United States Army. They have been sentenced to death by the Army and the Civil Authorities of Denver.' He eyed the frightened buffalo hunters. 'Hang them!'

The men were hurried forward by eager troopers and lifted on to waiting horses. The ropes hung down, roughly tied nooses swinging in the night wind as spooky ponies shuffled their hooves as nervously as the watching crowd.

'Wait!' It was Jubal who stepped out from the encircling ring of soldiers to question the condemned men. The troopers stood by the horses. 'Where's Riley? Do any of you know?'

'Go to hell.'

'Fucking renegade. He'll find you. An' I hope he kills you.'

Jubal stepped back to stand next to Simms.

'I guess I just don't have that bedside manner they all talk about,' he said bitterly, 'but I'd still like to know where Riley is.'

'You and me both,' replied the Army man, 'but I figure he'll show up sooner or later. Until then, we've got more immediate business.'

He lifted his sabre, glinting bright in the lamplight from the saloons and the hand-held lanterns of the crowd.

'Yo!'

The troopers stationed by the horses lashed gauntlets and rope-ends against the animals' withers and they rushed forwards across the street. Behind them, six men danced in the air, their boot heels drumming a soundless tattoo against nothing as their eyes bulged against bloodshot sockets and their tongues extended blackly into the night. They kicked and swung against the deadly pressure of the restraining ropes,

116

writhing an insane death dance in the empty air as the last vestiges of life choked out of their bodies.

One by one they fell silent as the final breath was dragged from blockèd lungs and the last sparks of life departed the dangling corpses.

Jubal watched impassively, more concerned with Riley's whereabouts than with the hanged men swinging from the saloon front. The Spencer rested in his arms, a cartridge in the chamber ready for the ex-peace officer, should he choose to make an appearance. But there was no sign of him.

'Let's go,' suggested Simms, 'we're finished here.'

'Yes,' Jubal replied, 'I guess we are. If it's all right with you I'll spend the night in camp and leave come morning.'

'Where for?' Simms asked.

'St. Louis. I was planning on going there before this trouble blew up. The boy I told you about — Andy Prescott — is there and it's a long time since I saw him.'

A long time and a lot of trouble, he thought as he fell into step beside the soldier, and too many corpses. It was over time he went back to check on Andy; the boy was alone in the world, with no one except Jubal, and totally dependent on the money the doctor could send for his care and his keep. Yes, it was about time he went back to St. Louis.

They returned to the cavalry bivouac and prepared to settle down for the night. The troopers were quiet now, their vengeance sated, the hot fury that had possessed them dissipated by the hanging and they, like Captain Simms, were satisfied that justice had been done. There would be no riot in Denver that night.

Jubal woke early the next day and enjoyed the sight of a spring sun bathing the snow-covered Plains with pale yellow light. The snow was clearing and the new season was so close he could almost smell it. He wondered what it would bring for the Cheyenne and if they would, as Big Wolf and Little Bear hoped, be able to live in peace on the Little Bighorn river. He hoped so and could see no reason why the whites should not allow the Indians this last, small piece of land to call their own. In any event, if the concentration of Sioux and Cheyenne was as large as Simms thought it seemed unlikely that any

117

sane soldier would dare attack them.

He shook off the strange feeling of foreboding that had crept over him and prepared coffee.

Simms was up a few minutes later and insisted on accompanying Jubal as he made his arrangements for the journey. Together, they rode to the bank, where Jubal withdrew the last of his funds to buy a rail ticket through to St. Louis. Then they went to the station where Jubal purchased a one-way ticket that would take him via Abilene and Kansas City over the thousand miles of metal that linked the Plains country to the Eastern towns along the Mississippi. The Kansas Pacific Railroad had one train scheduled that day, due to leave Denver at noon, and Jubal booked himself a sleeping berth. He had just enough money and did not relish the idea of travelling the whole distance in the high-backed, hard wood seats that were the common lot of passengers travelling shorter distances. When he reached St. Louis he hoped to find work to pay for Andy's fees at the Lenz Clinic, maybe even a chance to practise medicine.

With Simms an eager companion, he went back into the centre of town to eat lunch. It was early, so they stopped for a drink first in one of Denver's numerous saloons. They were sipping their whiskey when three men approached, Colt revolvers tied down on their hips and eyes flickering tensely between Jubal and the soldier.

Jubal's right hand was resting on his belt buckle in easy reach of the gun holstered beneath his coat as they came up to the bar.

'Doc,' mumbled the first man, 'you probably don't remember me.'

Jubal didn't.

'The name's Jesse. You took an arrow outta my shoulder that time with Riley. I wanted to say thanks.'

'Accepted,' grinned Jubal, exposing his broken teeth in a boyish smile as tension drained from his body. 'Glad you recovered.'

'This is Tad an' Charley,' the man continued, 'we got somethin' to tell you.'

'Yeah.' It was Charley. 'We figgered we owe you somethin' for what you did to patch Jesse. Heard somethin' that might help you.'

Tad broke in. 'What we want to say, doc, is that Les Riley figgers to hit you. He was swearin' it all the way back to Denver an' then again after the last time.'

'We weren't involved in that attack,' Charley said hurriedly, 'Riley was raisin' men to hit the Cheyenne but we didn't want no part of it.'

'Not after what the doc did for me,' added Jesse. 'But now it looks like Riley's aimin' to ambush you afore you leave.'

'Thanks for the warning,' Jubal said easily, although he felt the cold chill of anticipated killing steal down his spine. 'I'll keep my eyes open.'

'You do that, doc,' mumbled the buffalo hunters, 'reckon you're worth more than old Les.'

They left the saloon and Jubal turned to Simms.

'I guess Les is like an old dyke,' he said, 'once the crack shows you can't stop it coming.'

CHAPTER SIXTEEN

The high-stacked engine pulled into Denver thirty minutes after noon by Jubal's hunter, the steam whistle mounted above the cow-catcher blasting a shrill warning to unwary passengers. Porters slung baggage into the windowless freight cars as the travellers climbed aboard. Captain Simms stood with his hands clasped behind his back as Jubal mounted the short metal ladder of an observation car, ignoring the bustle around him.

'Good luck, Jubal Cade. You tried to do something worthwhile out here. It wasn't your fault it didn't come off.'

Jubal shrugged from his vantage point on the rear platform.

'Before that happens,' he grinned, 'we'll need to unite the nations, not just the states.'

The long, black train blew a last lonely whistle as it pulled out of Denver and Jubal bade a final goodbye to the tall figure of the soldier as the shallow platform faded into the distance. He turned and made his way through the crowded carriages to the berth where a porter had stowed his gear. He checked his black medical bag and then the Spencer rifle, stashed his saddlebags under the bunk and lowered himself on to the mattress. With a sigh of contentment he closed his eyes, allowing himself to drift down into sleep.

He awoke later that afternoon and, mindful of the warning, worked his way from one end of the train to the other, watching for Les Riley. He saw no sign of the vengeful marshal among the short-stop passengers, nor any in the restaurant car or bar waggon. And although it was impossible to check the people travelling in the locked sleeping berths, Jubal felt easier in his mind as he made his way at dusk to the eats waggon.

His keen brown eyes scanned the figures seated on either

120

side of the long, swaying carriage as he allowed a Negro waiter to usher him to a table. There, he joined two cattlemen and a solitary lady schoolteacher more intent on their food than on entering into conversation with the rather travel-stained young man who joined them. Towards the end of the meal, however, the ranchers expressed an interest in poker and Jubal's ears pricked up at the mention of his favourite game. Slipping easily into the politely unassuming manner that belied his essential ruthlessness, he talked the cattlemen into asking him to sit in.

They played into the early hours of the morning with Jubal taking the better part of a hundred dollars in winnings.

The ranchers were yawning as they threw in their hands, ruefully admitting that they had underestimated the skill of the black-haired man who had quietly and consistently taken their money. Jubal was pleased with the game. He enjoyed it anyway, and if he was able to build up his stake so easily, he enjoyed it all the more. They retired to the ever-open saloon car for a nightcap before agreeing to meet again the following day for another session. Jubal made his way back to his berth, carefully locking the flimsy door before he stripped off his clothing and climbed into the bunk.

The next morning he shaved in the bowl of hot water delivered by the same cheerful Negro who had seated him at dinner, spruced up as best he could in the close confines of the sleeper, and then began to dress.

He pulled on his last clean shirt, knotting a thin black tie around the white collar, then hung the shoulder rig that carried the re-modelled ·30 calibre Colt against his chest, covering the leather straps with the grey vest made, like the rest of his suit, in the far-off days when he had studied medicine in England. He checked the gold hunter watch – it read 7.00 a.m. – and hung it carefully over the vest. Like the Spencer rifle, the watch was one of Jubal's few prized possessions: something he really cared about. He pushed his arms into the grey jacket of the suit, set his derby on his head and left the berth.

He opened the door slowly, eyes checking the empty corridor, then began to walk up the rolling carriage towards the restaurant car.

Four doors back cold eyes watched him from the slit of a partially opened sleeper.

Jubal made his way up to the restaurant car and ordered breakfast, sipping happily on the strong black coffee that was served as he sat down beside the schoolmarm he had met the night before. In the light of morning she proved more willing to talk, revealing that she had spent the last six months on an Indian reservation, teaching Sioux and Cheyenne to speak American.

'It is not,' she told Jubal with disapproval written across her face, 'like Washington. Home, that is. They simply do not wish to learn our language.'

'Do they have one of their own?' he asked innocently.

'Well,' she snorted in disgust at the backwardness of the uncultured savages, 'they do grunt at one another. But it is not, without doubt, what one might call a *proper* language.'

'Did you ever think, ma'am,' Jubal asked, 'that they might not want to learn English?'

'Honestly,' replied Miss Willes, her reliable Washington background jumping to the fore, 'they *must*. We can hardly converse with them in that odd collection of sounds *they* call speech.'

'Funny thing is, ma'am,' said Jubal, beginning to enjoy his gentle needling, 'that they might just feel the same way about us. That's something you might think about.'

'Well, really,' snorted Miss Willes, 'if that's what you think.'

Her sentence was punctuated by the sudden crash of a heavy calibre gun. She screamed as splinters of wood exploded from the back of her seat and threw herself down between the chair and the table.

Jubal had powered himself out into the aisle at the sound of the shot, rolling between the legs of shouting, screaming, running passengers. His right hand snaked, lightning-fast under his jacket, hauling the big Colt clear of the holster and thumbing back the hammer in one clean movement. He ended up beneath a table that spilled coffee and fresh bread over his suit as the occupants scattered in panic.

A second bullet ploughed a long furrow down the centre of the car, ricocheting upwards into the back of a running diner. The man clutched at his spine, yelling as the burning lead destroyed his nerve centres, and pitched forward across a full table. His weight tore the thing loose from its mountings, so that it toppled into the central walkway, affording Jubal the cover he needed.

With one swift rush, he powered himself up and out from between the seats to land in a cat-deadly crouch behind the overturned table.

At the far end of the diner he saw Les Riley, a smoking Colt in his right hand coming up to fire again.

'I told you, Cade,' he shouted as the gun bellowed for the third time, 'I wouldn't let you go. You mean too much.'

Jubal triggered his own gun and saw the bullet blast flakes of Kansas Pacific veneer over Riley's greying hair.

'As I said once before,' he yelled, 'it's nice to know you're wanted.'

Riley snarled and hauled off another shot, the shell smashing through the thin planking that was Jubal's only cover.

The car was empty now, the passengers fled to the safety of the farther carriage, where doors were firmly bolted against the two madmen fighting their savage duel within the breakfast waggon, their only witness the dead man sprawled across the aisle.

Jubal realized that there was no way out other than through Riley. Yet the marshal was hidden behind the seats at the far end of the car, sheltered by tables and upturned chairs, his back firmly set against the only exit. Jubal eyed the new battleground, then came to a swift decision.

'Riley!' he yelled, 'if you want me you'll have to come after me.'

He pushed the Colt into its holster as he shouted, and picked up the fallen table in powerful arms. With a single movement, he hurled the wooden bulk through the window on his left side. The table shattered the glass, flying through on to the snow beyond. Jubal followed it, powering his body up and out through the broken glass. He felt shards pluck at his jacket as he clutched the upper, curved window-frame, fingers finding desperate purchase on the cold wood. Then he was swinging outwards, legs flailing to find balance.

It came as the train swung around a curve that threw Riley's next shot off target, giving Jubal the time he needed to clamber on to the roof. He pulled himself into the centre where a double-line of handholds, slightly raised above the ceiling, aided his progress down the car.

He crawled on, feeling the lines of naked anger pull his face into the mask of hatred that he knew overcame him when faced with someone such as Riley. Behind him, bullets smashed through the roof, marking his passage with a line of ragged holes. Yet he ignored both the danger of Riley's shots and the tugging of the wind that threatened to tear him from the swaying train in his determination to end the fight once and for all.

The firing ended as Riley emptied his gun and paused to reload.

Jubal took the opportunity to swing down off the roof on to the observation platform, his own gun jumping into his hand as he landed.

He sprang to one side of the door as it flew open, revealing the snarling face of the marshal, his finger squeezing the trigger as he kicked through the door.

'Sorry, Riley,' Jubal murmured as he fired his own gun, 'but you don't give me much choice.'

The ·30 calibre bullet blasted a hole through Riley's stomach that sprayed blood out over the following carriage. The renegade marshal screamed, dropping his Colt as he clutched at the burning pain in his belly. Blood-flecked spittle clotted in his moustache as he doubled over, his hands pressed against the agony flooding through his body.

'Damn you, Cade,' he spat through the bright, red blood that dribbled over his lips and chin, 'I coulda made it to that ranch. You were the down payment.'

He broke off as waves of raw agony washed over him, through him, numbing his tenuous grip on life so that he slid, slowly, over the edge of the platform. Mumbling bloodily, he clung to the metal floor, pain-racked eyes staring up at Jubal.

'You were the payload. You just wouldn't die like I planned.'

Jubal looked down at the broken man. 'I guess you should have left my death up to me,' he said, lifting his foot.

He brought it down on Riley's fingers, feeling the bones break as he watched the hand slip away from the platform. For a moment, the killer marshal clung to the carriage with his one remaining hand, then that lost its grip and he slid under the next car.

He screamed once as the wheels went over him. After that the snow-covered land was silent except for the train noises as the big locomotive carried Jubal towards St. Louis.

He turned back to the empty carriage.

'I'm coming back, Andy,' he murmured as the frightened passengers began to enter the car, 'and maybe this time it's for keeps.'

He paused to pick up a scrap of paper that blew down the aisle from the now-deserted observation platform. He looked at it, deciphering the words on the crumpled sheet: DESCRIPTION FITS. DELIVER CADE OR CERTIFICATE OF DEATH. REWARD YOURS. It was signed AGNEW.

'Yes,' muttered Jubal Cade, 'one way or another I'm coming back.'

showed no sign of infection; he felt weak, but that was only to be expected and nothing that a few days' more rest and a reasonable diet could not cure. For a week longer he took things easy, lying outside his tepee as Little Bear's wife brought him food, talking with the Cheyenne who now flocked to speak to him through the translations of his two friends.

At last, when he was fully recovered, Big Wolf approached. The chief wanted Jubal to ride into Denver and contact the authorities. He hoped that a white man might succeed where Indians had failed in persuading the powers-that-be of the good intentions of the Cheyenne and the indignities they had suffered at the hands of the white people.

Jubal agreed. He had been heading for Denver anyway so it was no hardship to continue his journey. Especially as Big Wolf offered him two saddlebags filled with the yellow metal that was drawing miners like flies to the honey-pot of the Black Hills. Jubal had little knowledge of gold-mining but still estimated that the two bags contained something in the region of a thousand dollars' worth of gold: enough to ensure Andy Prescott's fees for several months. So he waited until the last of the mid-winter blizzards had cleared and set out.

The foothills of the Rockies were still covered with snow that blanketed the great open spaces with blinding white, broken only by the stark black trunks of the great fir trees rearing up through the drifts. He was accompanied as far as the frozen banks of the South Platte River by a group of seven warriors led by Little Bear. They left him by the river with a packhorse loaded with supplies and instructions to follow the river south into Denver.

Jubal promised again to carry their message to the authorities and return himself, if he could, with the answer. Otherwise he would endeavour to get a message through by some other means.

Little Bear assured Jubal that he would be welcome in the Cheyenne territory at any time and, clearly sorry to see his friend depart alone, turned his pony west and rode off through the snow. Jubal turned his own mount south and led the packhorse behind him down the edge of the river. He rode for two days without seeing any sign of another being alive

35

in the bleak, winter-crusted landscape. His only companions were the two horses, their nostrils spuming jets of steam into the freezing air as they ploughed slowly on through the deep snowdrifts. The going was arduous and Jubal was forced to make frequent detours whenever the snow became too deep to negotiate. He had only the river and the pale sun to steer by and was required to make fairly frequent side-trips to find the South Platte whenever he was pushed away from it by deep snow. He realized that he could get easily lost in the snowfields of the High Plains country and drift aimlessly until his food ran out if he did not keep the river on his left, so he stayed close even though it meant he would probably take longer to reach Denver.

His first sight of the town came on the third day. Columns of wispy smoke stood straight up above the plain and the deep snow began to recede under the impact of numerous wagon tracks. Jubal rode on, relishing the thought of a hot bath and a soft bed. And, more than anything else, the taste of a cheroot.

He pushed on through the steadily clearing snow until he drew level with the town. Like most western settlements it was a ragged sprawl of wooden buildings, few reaching higher than a single storey although four or five boasted a third level and about a dozen of the structures reached two floors. It was the first town of any size Jubal had seen since leaving Laredo and the biggest gathering of buildings since St. Louis. Standing up squat and smoky out of the bare white plain it looked like an ugly jumble of children's building blocks dropped carelessly on to a clean white cloth.

But the aspect of white civilization carried little concern for Jubal at that moment. His more immediate problem was getting across the river. The South Platte was running too fast at this point for any reliable thickness of surface ice to form and Jubal was wary of trusting the pack-ice crusting the surface of the river. On the far bank he spotted the low outline of a ferry and yelled across. A figure, bulky in winter clothing emerged from a small hut beside the landing stage and began to haul the floating platform through the water by means of a long rope secured to either bank and connected to the